MUAWZA

THE COMPENSATION
and Other Stories

Author of The Year Nominee, 2021 by Story Mirror

SANJIV PRIYADARSHI

Copyright © Sanjiv Priyadarshi 2023
All Rights Reserved.

ISBN 979-8-88883-985-0

This book has been published with all efforts taken to make the material error-free after the consent of the author. However, the author and the publisher do not assume and hereby disclaim any liability to any party for any loss, damage, or disruption caused by errors or omissions, whether such errors or omissions result from negligence, accident, or any other cause.

While every effort has been made to avoid any mistake or omission, this publication is being sold on the condition and understanding that neither the author nor the publishers or printers would be liable in any manner to any person by reason of any mistake or omission in this publication or for any action taken or omitted to be taken or advice rendered or accepted on the basis of this work. For any defect in printing or binding the publishers will be liable only to replace the defective copy by another copy of this work then available.

*In fond memories of my parents who made me
what I am.*

*To my adorable wife Plabita and my children Shailee
and Akshat; my brightest stars.*

CONTENTS

INTRODUCTION

In my long stint as a law enforcement officer, events encountered in my personal and professional lives have been inspiring me to closely watch and bring out the underlying emotions and exploits of people around us and pen them down. But life is one and distractions are many. So it happened one morning while I was shuffling through the endless forwards of 'Good Morning' messages on my phone when a template caught my eyes. It read, "Go to the other end of this universe to do and get what you want in life". I thought it over and said to myself, 'Well, I have to type just a letter; my resignation, and I am there!' And that is how this collection was borne.

To be honest, aptly describing the genre of this book would be a little difficult as the stories have sprouted on different soils and in different climates, but they are all intense and alive; happening and growing around us, drawing their sap from their characters and blossoming into myriad of colours of emotions, pain, desperation, remorse and love being the primary hues.

Please allow me to admit that I am not a professional writer and this being my debut collection published in print, errors are but natural and I apologise for the same.

Let's begin.

* *

MUAWZA

*Compensation for a loss seldom compensates,
for unlike gain, the quantum of the loss can
never be measured!*

The dark row of tiny shanties along the highway was gearing up for another night. Half naked children with hungry bellies scampered around the make shift ovens around the settlement; greedily waiting for the food. The air was torrid with smoke from the ovens and burning garbage. Some of the dwellers had already laid mats and rugs on the dusty sidewalk for the night. It was just another evening in the slum, sprawled on the outskirts of the city; stretching for almost a mile.

Haria turned restlessly on his rug and stared into the dark starry night. His looked at his daughter Jamuna woith his failing eyes, sleeping on her rug alongside and sighed. It was now almost a year since his son Krishna had left home. His disappearance had shattered his heart and hopes of better days. Jamuna was almost near marriageable age and this thought made him more restive and desperate every passing day. He closed his eyes and tried to sleep.

They suddenly woke up with frightening sound of screeching tyres and a large thud which was followed by shouts and screams of people. Beside her, Jamuna had also woken up in panic. There was a big commotion around and people were running and screaming. Amid the chaos, Haria could make out that a truck had veered off the road and ploughed onto the pavement and into the tenements; crushing sleeping people. He tottered along with others to the truck and looked with horror. His old neighbour Velu, who was sleeping outside his shanty next door, was crushed under the front wheel of the truck and had died instantly. A few other men sleeping on the sidewalk were injured. A big crowd had gathered at the site and everyone was screaming. By this time they had caught the scared driver and began thrashing him. Almost after an hour, police arrived at the scene and took the battered driver in custody. Ambulances arrived much later; with sirens blaring, and ferried the dead body of Velu and the injured, leaving behind wailing women and children.

Like most others in the slum, Haria and Jamuna too could not sleep for the rest of the night. Children, still shaken by the accident, sat in a group silently with sleep laden eyes. The women whose shanties were destroyed by the impact were picking up their belongings and broken utensils from the debris, cursing their fate for the misfortune. A pall of gloom had descended on the slum. Haria and Jamuna, robbed of sleep, huddled on their rugs and waited for the night to end.

A couple of weeks later, a big caravan of cars and police vehicles arrived at the slum. An imposing middle aged man clad in whites got down from the leading car, surrounded by his cronies. He was the local MLA. Soon, everyone from the slum gathered around them. Those who remained indifferent were coaxed by his accomplices and police men to attend the 'ceremony'. After the MLA was garlanded by his deputy, he cleared his throat and announced how the fateful incident in the slum; which was nothing less than his family, had shaken and hurt him. He expressed his gratitude for their support in the last election and promised that he would continue fighting for the rights and betterment of the slum dwellers since they had voted for him. After singing a long self -praise, he paused and told one of his men to fetch the wife of the old man who had died in the accident. The slum dwellers looked with awe as they respectfully escorted Velu's widow to the makeshift dais. The MLA bowed down and touched the feet of the bewildered woman. After posing with her for the camera, he took out a piece of paper and handed over to her which he proudly announced to the crowd that it was a cheque for Rs. two lakhs as 'Muawza' for Velu's death. There was an uproarious gasp in awe and applause from the slum dwellers who scrambled to get a view of the cheque. The MLA went on to boast how he had to fight with the administration to get that amount sanctioned for the family. After finishing his speech, he posed pompously with the shaken woman holding the cheque in her hand and smiled at the photographer. He also announced to the overwhelmed crowd that he would take all necessary steps for their safety in future and vowed a harsh punishment to the errant driver.

After he had left, Haria and other slum dwellers gathered around Velu's wife to get a glimpse of the cheque and congratulate her. No one in the slum had ever seen an amount as big as that. They congratulated her for the 'windfall' and praised God and the MLA for the bounty. A woman commended Velu's noble soul and uttered how he had taken care of the old woman even after his death by getting the money for her. She rued that Velu was too sick anyway and would not have lived much longer even without the accident. Haria too felt happy for the widow who was handicapped and too old to work for a living.

In coming days, life limped back to normal in the slum. The injured had come back; overwhelmed by the free treatment and sumptuous food in the hospital. Sitting in groups, they chatted excitedly about the 'royal' treatment they had received in hospital which included three meals in a day with desserts and the muwaza Velu's wife had received.

As the days passed, Haria turned more desolate by the memories of Krishna as hopes of his return diminished. His desperation and agony were worsened by the accident and his friend Velu's death. In dark and lonely nights, he searched for his only hope, his son; in the streaks of light from the falling stars. Every night he lay silently, gaping at the dark expanse of sky; with sleepless eyes, crying silently. His solitude in the company of a million stars above him haunted him when he gazed at them with his opaque eyes.

It was yet another hot and humid night in the slum. The highway was busy as usual with vehicles zooming past; spewing fumes and raising tiny storms of dust after them. The glare of the headlights from passing vehicles sliced the row of shanties every few seconds,; like the beam of a lighthouse spearing the expanse of dark seas. His eyes chased the tail lights of every passing vehicle; in hope that someday, one would stop and he would see his son again. He closed his eyes and tried to sleep.

Suddenly a frightening thought startled him. Drenched in sweat and panic, he sat up on his bed, palpitating. With his head hung on his frail chest, he pondered for a long time. And then he smirked, shaking his head in the darkness, as if assuring himself. He looked at Jamuna's silhouette who was asleep on her rug nearby and made up his mind. At that very moment, he saw a pair of headlights slowly rolling down on the highway. It looked like a big truck. He fixed his sight on the highway. He was ready.

Krishna was ecstatic. Perched on the driving seat of his truck, he could feel the tremble in his fingers wrapped around the steering wheel; thinking of his father and Jamuna. He could see their bewildered and smiling faces swimming in front of his eyes; when he would wake them up and surprise with the gifts he had bought for them. After fleeing home, he had worked hard through the year to make this happen and tonight he would change their fate! The thoughts of Jamuna's 'grand' wedding and a *pucca* room with a cot for his father were swelling in his chest.

He was almost there. Now he could see the familiar rooflines of the slum where he had grown up. 'Nothing has really changed,' he smiled to himself. Tears welled in his eyes as he spotted his shanty in the dark; just a few yards away. He tried to compose himself and wiped his eyes. Slowing down the truck, he switched off the headlights so as not to alert them before his surprise. At that moment, a shadow jumped from nowhere before his massive truck. He tried to steer away but it was too late as his reflexes were impacted by his intense emotions and thoughts. The next moment, he heard the nerve chilling sound of cracking bones beneath the weight of his massive truck and an agonising cry of death which sounded too familiar.

Amidst the cries and shouts of people, Krishna jumped out of the driver's cabin. With sinking heart, he leaned on the blood soaked face of the dying old man. Even in the darkness, he could recognise the battered face, the pale frozen eyes and those dry weathered lips which were feebly murmuring: 'Muawza, Muawza.'

* *

PORIMA

*Pain is perpetual; like the molten lava, waiting
in the deep caverns of a volcano.*

The boat sailed lazily on the vast expanse of the magnificent Brahmaputra. A sudden gush of cool wind blew my hair as I looked into the calm waters below. It had the tinge of red from a late evening sun. Young children playing on the white sandy banks of the river waived at us jubilantly. I smiled and waived back at them as we sailed into the wind which carried fragrance of fresh water and wet sand. It was a pleasant November afternoon and I was thoroughly enjoying the boat ride with my friends who had come with me from Atlanta to this trip of North East India. They had been pestering me for years to take them to my home town of Tezpur and other tourist spots in the state.

Shisir the boatman, who was also our local guide, was at the helm, singing a folk song passionately.

I could not understand his dialect, but could make out that it was a happy one.

'What is the meaning of the song?' I shouted to him over the noise of the boat engine.

'A *Bihu* (a major festival of Assam) song, *Bideu* (sister); it says that today is the day when you see someone who has been waiting for a long time to meet you whom you forgot long ago.' He smiled shyly. I translated it to my curious friends who exclaimed in unison, 'How romantic!' and resumed clicking pictures of the river and half naked kids on the sun bathed shore.

'Beautiful, isn't it?' the boatman pointed to a grove of tall trees bathed in crimson, partly camouflaging a small settlement behind the setting sun. It looked like a village on the river banks, still far away. From a distance, I could see the traditional Assam styled houses made of bamboos and thatched roofs; dotted among areca and palm trees.

'That is *Mangaldoi*.' He pointed out non-emphatically to the small settlement on the peninsula and continued sailing.

I froze, my gaze fixed on the shore where a tiny dust storm had partly clouded the shoreline and the village behind it.

'*Mangaldoi*!' I gasped.

'It is a small village, nothing much to see there, Bideu!' Shisir ignored my expression and resumed his singing.

The name mixed with the sound of gushing wind reverberated in my ears; making me dizzy. The memories and faces forgotten long ago came alive and began to surface on the tranquil waters of the river around me! Among those memories, a tiny face emerged, flanked by a pair of beaded ear rings and a broad smile on small, pink lips. I shuddered with the shock of this sudden remembrance!

'Porima,'I whispered!

10 years ago, Mumbai.

It was a lazy Saturday morning and I was still in bed, my head aching from a mild hangover from the party last night. Sanjay was up and glued to his newspaper on the patio when the telephone rang at the bed side. I whined in my pillow and picked up the phone reluctantly.

'Hi! Natasha here. Don't tell me it is too early but I need you guys here to see someone.' She almost ordered.

I whimpered in protest, 'Hey, it is too early and that too on a Saturday!"

'No, no excuses, we are meeting over lunch here, that's it.' She disconnected before I could refuse. It was difficult to say no to Natasha. She knew the art of persuasion which sometimes worked in her favour in fund collection drives for her NGO. I liked her, although I was not very comfortable visiting her sanatorium which was a shelter for children from poor families who came from distant corners of country for treatment of cancer and other difficult diseases and depended on her NGO for stay in Bombay and funding their treatment; if needed. Their sight and sufferings unsettled me and therefore I avoided being there.

We arrived at her office in her sanatorium late afternoon. After having lunch, Natasha called for her assistant who ushered a couple in their late thirties and a little shy girl who was trying to hide behind them. The couple, hesitant and overwhelmed, sat on the chairs across us. The little girl, wearing a floral frock and a hand knit cap on her head, stood between her parents, clinging to the coarse 'mekhla chador' (traditional *Assames* variant of saree) her mother wore, looking curiously at us, blinking her tiny blue eyes.

'Partha, meet Pallavi and Sanjay. Pallavi is from Assam, your state,' Natasha addressed the man and introduced us. The man beamed, emboldened by meeting someone from his native state in an alien city and got up from his chair to greet us. He had a thin frame and looked worried and beaten. He told us that they came from *Mangaldoi*, a small village near *Tezpur*.

'And this is our little star Porima, the fairy queen,' Natasha smiled at the girl who was clinging to her mother. Turning in my chair, I smiled and looked at her closely. She was about six years old and had sharp features and stunningly beautiful blue eyes. A pair of oversized ear rings studded with cheap red stones hung on her tiny ears which touched her pale cheeks and clinked as she shook her head.

Natasha summoned her assistant again who took Porima and her mother out. Then she turned to me and said, 'Porima has a tumour in her brain. They treated her in Guwahati but the doctors advised them to take to Mumbai for advance treatment;

so they are here. I have spoken to the doctors in Tata Memorial Hospital and fixed an appointment for her. The treatment is going to be expensive and they can't afford it. 'Partha needs help and that is the reason I called you! Can you sponsor her? '

With corners of his eyes, Partha looked expectantly at us; helplessness and shame of asking writ large on his face. I was shocked. 'How it is possible! She is but a lovely little child!,' I murmured.

'The appointment with the specialist is due on Monday,' Natasha addressed her father reassuringly who sat with a sullen face and looked at me expectantly.

We immediately agreed to sponsor her treatment. Over the next few minutes we discussed the arrangements for their stay, transport and funds. The conversation was making me heady and unnerved. Leaving Sanjay with Partha and Natasha, I got up and came out of her office, where I found Porima and her mother waiting on a bench. Porima tottered hesitantly to me and raised her blue eyes, 'Ma told that you speak *Assames*?' her voice was sweet and steady.

'Yes my dear, I can.' I smiled at her and held her tiny finger.

'And Ma also told that you would be coming to meet and play with me here, would you?' her blue eyes were curious.

'Yes, sweetheart, I will and let me see your earrings, they are really pretty.' I bent down and lightly kissed her on her cheeks. She blushed and ran back to the side of her mother.

Over next few weeks, we began seeing Porima more frequently as her treatment began. As part of our commitment, Sanjay and I took turns to ferry Porima and her parents to the hospital and consult her doctors whenever required. In coming weeks, my bonding with Porima grew as I began spending more time with her in the sanatorium and the hospital and brought little gifts for her. She loved flashy costume jewellery and stuffed toys. She also wrote letters in unsteady words; to her teacher and friends in the village which I would take to post. One day while I was reading her a book, she held my hand and whispered, 'Are you adopting me?' I was taken aback and laughed aloud.

'No, who told you this? I wish I could, but you have your Papa and Ma who love you so much! How can I take you away from them!' I laughed and hugged her.

'Have you read Lord Krishna's story?' Unfazed, she dared me, shaking her bandaged head.

'No, I haven't, why?' I teased her, mimicking her mischievous voice.

She picked up a story book from her bed I had bought for her. 'See, I read it here; she clutched my fingers and moved them on the prints and read, 'The evil Kansa wanted to kill Krishna, but Ma *Yashoda* adopted him and took him with her, away from Kansa so that she could save him. In the same way, if you adopt me, you can save me from my Kansa.' She said pointing her finger at her bandaged crown covered by a cap.

I turned my face away from her to hide my pain.

Porima did not ask that question after that day; she had probably sensed that I was not comfortable with that conversation.

A few days later, Natasha broke the frightening news. Porima's biopsy reports had come which confirmed that the tumour was malignant.

'She would have to be in the hospital for a longer period for chemotherapy and surgery, if necessary.'

she grimaced. I was shattered! For the first time, I was scared for Porima.

A week later, sitting by her bed in the hospital, I tried to look courageous. She had lost weight; her tiny body ravaged by cancer and the chemicals injected in her tiny body. She was asleep but when I touched her fingers, she opened her eyes and smiled at me.

'Now tell me when you are going to adopt me' she said mischievously in a weak and breaking voice.

I ran to the door of the ward as my tears broke. When I returned to her bed after composing myself, she whispered in my ears, '*Khuri* (Aunty), I am sorry, you are angry at me, aren't you? It was just a joke! I would never say that again, promise!'

My heart broke. I hugged her and cried, burying my tears in her bosom.

She was discharged from the hospital in a few days and recuperated in the sanatorium; waiting for her next round of chemotherapy. Now I was seeing her more frequently and even took her to nearby malls where we ate ice cream and candy floss and shopped for her.During one pf the trips to the mall, I bought her a huge teddy bear which she adored.

Next month, the big news came! Sanjay and I were assigned new roles by our company in Atlanta, USA which we had been looking forward to. It was my dream job but somehow I was not as enthusiastic about it then. Porima had returned from the hospital after her third round of chemotherapy. Her doctors had advised her to stay for a few more weeks in the city to complete her last cycle of chemotherapy and the subsequent surgery. As our travel date neared, I began seeing her almost every day in the hospital or sanatorium. I wanted to be at her side at the time of surgery but it looked impossible as the date of our travel was just a few days away.

Before leaving, we had made sure that her treatment was not compromised for lack of funds. Sanjay had also arranged a part time accounting job for Partha. We went to see Porima a day before we flew to USA. I sat on her bed and kissed her and whispered in her ears, 'Once I come back, I shall adopt you.' She smiled and remained silent, clutching my fingers hard; her mute eyes fixed on me, as if telling me not to go.

The new job was tough on both of us. Natasha kept me informed of Porima's progress though I always suspected that she was not too optimistic about her. A few weeks later, she mailed me that her surgery was successful and that they had left for their village. She also mailed me a photograph of Porima with a broad smile on her face; hugging the teddy bear. In coming days, I tried to call Partha on the number Natasha had given me but the calls could not go through. Memories of Porima gradually faded away in the obscurities of work and the busy American life as the years passed!

Standing in the centre of the boat with my gaze fixed on the settlement on the river bank, I was oblivious of my friends' giggles and laughs. Pointing to the shore towards the cluster of houses in the village, I commanded Shisir, 'Take us to *Mangaldoi*.'

Partha's telephone number was still saved in my cell phone. With excited fingers, I dialled the landline phone which went unanswered. By this time the bewildered boatman had moored the boat and was standing in the galley, waiting for us to step out;, wondering why we were there. I settled my friends in a make shift tea stall on the river bank and headed for the village, which was about a hundred yards away ; walking through the serpentine pathways.

After asking a few people in the street, I reached a nondescript decaying house at the dead end of a narrow lane. It had bare brick walls and a roof thatched with dried elephant grass. With pounding heart, I knocked at the rickety door of the house, which opened after a long wait. Even after all those years, I instantly recognised Partha who awkwardly stood in the doorway, wearing a vest and a lion cloth. He had shrunk and looked pale and desolate. For a few moments, he looked at me with blank eyes; trying to remember and then gasped with disbelief. Silently, he ushered me in.

'Porima?' I mumbled, gathering my courage.

His voice shivered, '*Bideu*, after you went to America, doctors operated on her tumour and said that they had done their best. They told us to take her home. She did well for some time but her condition worsened very quickly.' His voice choked.

The world around me began crumbling into pieces. The surge of fear and remorse hibernating for years suddenly rose and slapped me in my face. I went numb; my legs buckling under the weight of my guilt and culpability.

'And her mother? Where is she?' My voice trembled with fear and trepidation.

Partha's eyes swelled with tears of pain. 'She too could not live long after Porima was gone, five years back......' his words again choked in his throat.

I was devastatingly silent, holding my tears! In a corner of the room, plastic toys and dolls of different sizes and colours were neatly stacked on a table. Among them was the big teddy bear, sitting upright, smiling at me, its furry arms stretched, as if inviting me for a hug!

'She would talk about you everyday. A week before she left us, she wrote this letter to you and told me to send to you but I did not have your address!' He went to the table and picked up a manila envelope tucked in the furry arms of the teddy bear.

With trembling fingers, I opened the envelope and unfolded the letter. The paper had yellowed by age. With sinking heart, I read silently. She had scribbled in unsteady words:

'Khuri,

Hope you are fine. *Deota* (Father) tells me that you have gone very far away, so I am writing this letter. Hope it reaches you. I am sure that you would come someday to meet me.

Do you remember the story of Lord Krishna and our joke? But now I know that it was not a joke. Trust me, I will not die if you adopt me like Ma *Yashoda* adopted little Krishna. I shall wait, but may be I have not much time, so come fast.

So Long,

Yours,

Porima'.

She had drawn a smiling face with a cap under her signature in red.

I squeezed the letter in my palm and closed my eyes!

* *

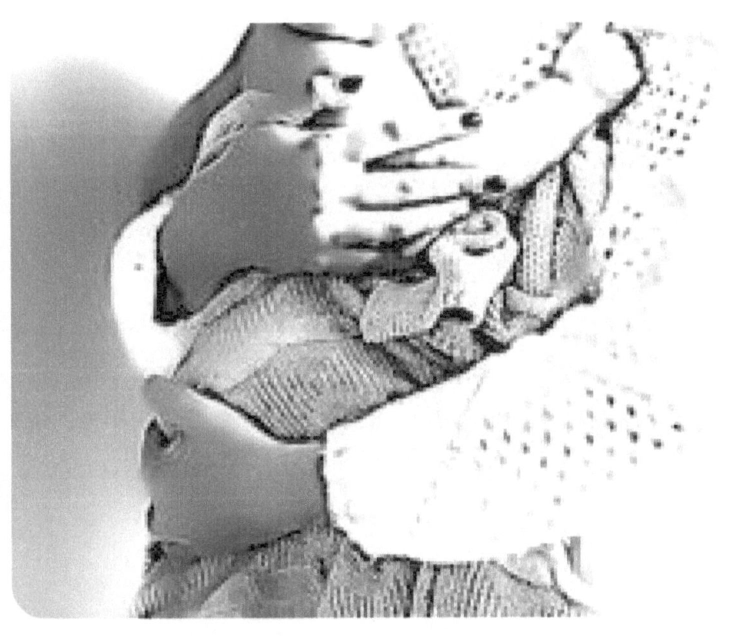

LET'S BEGIN AFRESH

Treachery and thanklessness can win a war, but can they vanquish a mother's longings to relive her joy of giving!

Clutching the small duffle bag, I looked at that house for the last time and sighed before settling down on the bench in the bus shelter. That house was my universe, my abode of happiness and sorrows, an expanse of sweet and bitter memories which we had made, brick by brick; where I had spent my life with Shuklaji and our only son Amit, the centre of our cosmos.

My universe had collapsed the day when Shuklaji breathed his last. His struggle with cancer and concern for me lurking in his dying eyes had been haunting me since then. Somehow I had hung on thin threads of his memories but I was desolate, like a river robbed of its flow and my heart a void like a giant black hole which had sucked my own existence. But this was still my world, my universe which was once my playground of longings and endearments!

With closed eyes, I waited for the bus. Images from the past began rolling like small boats riding on turbulent waves; vanishing behind big surges and re-emerging only to be drowned again by another wave. They zoomed past me in split second deceptions like optical illusions of a mirage in desert, appearing in front of my half closed eyes, only to dissipate the next moment.

A few weeks after Shuklaji's death, Amit had come to me and rued how his father's ailment had drenched him financially. With a little hesitation, he suggested that I might consider shifting with my brother in our village where I could be 'happier'.

'Amma, this house is small and Mamaji too had been insisting that you settle down with them in the village.' Amit sounded apologetic. His words, though soft, shattered my heart like a strong gush of wind wrecking a paper boat on choppy waters!

'My son, I have spent my life here and it is painful to think leaving you and memories of this house!' I protested feebly. He had nodded his head in dismay and left.

Although, after that day Amit never repeated his proposal to shift me from our home, I could feel the subdued unrest in the house. In coming days, Amit and his wife Madhu grew more restless and irritable, often fighting each other over trivial issues. That house, Amit and Madhu and their yet to be borne child meant everything to me and I shuddered at the thought of going away from them. Several days passed while I cried in my pillow on the thought of leaving that little piece of world left to me.

One morning while shifting the pages of the newspaper, I saw an advert of a 'Retiring Home for seniors'. It boasted of 'Dignified living in golden age' and 'A family away from family' with a picture of smiling, happy and inviting wrinkled faces. That was the day I had decided to move to an old age home. 'With my pension, I could live there with dignity, and Amit and Madhu could also have their privacy;' I had assured myself.

Amit was taken aback! 'How can you think of old age home, Amma,' he looked offended. 'And have you thought of what people would say!' He snapped! But I had decided.

A few months after Madhu had delivered their child, I told Amit that my decision to move to the old age home was final and in better interest of all. The very next day, I called that old age home which was in a nearby city and spoke to the manager who assured me that he would reserve a place for me when I arrive.

And now, there I was, waiting for the bus which would take me to my new abode, a new chapter in my life, probably the last one! Amit had insisted to come with me but I refused. 'Do not worry, I will manage, you must stay with Madhu and the child.' I was firm.

Amit stood by my side silently; where I sat on the cold stone bench of the bus stop. The bus arrived. Amit picked up my suitcase. 'Amma, do not worry, I will be coming to see you regularly, and we can talk on phone anytime; ok?' He meekly smiled. I avoided looking into his eyes; lest I found any tears of remorse or separation, if there were any. Madhu touched my feet, murmuring something apologetically which I could not hear. I took the infant from her lap and kissed him. He was a replica of Amit, dark eyes and cute little dimples in his pink cheeks. 'I will come on your first birthday,' I promised in his tiny ears and boarded the bus, holding back my tears. From my window, I waived back to them and to the house.

With my vision blurred with moisture, the house looked like swinging and waiving back at me as the bus drove away. Next to me sat a young mother with a fussing infant on her lap, breastfeeding her and singing a lullaby in a hushed tone. The past began swimming in the wells of my eyes. I thought of Amit, whom I had never kept away from myself for a single day in my life. I closed my eyes and thought of him. My eyelids were becoming heavy with the weight of pain and remorse of parting away from my world.

In my slumber, I dreamt of my little Amit, clung to my bosom. I wished I could freeze that moment for ever! In the next frame of my dream, I was whispering to him in my delirium, 'My son, where did I go wrong! Did not I put you on my bosom and feed you my sap? Didn't I vow to shed my blood in return of your tears when you were sick; or burn my youth for the pink of your cheeks and keep awake through the nights to make you sleep! Did I ever fail in rejoicing in your happiness and crying in your pain or did I not shiver in the cruel cold nights to keep you warm!'

I woke up with a jolt which shattered my dream. The bus had arrived at my destination. It was a pleasant midmorning. A gentle blow of cool air welcomed me as I got down from the bus. I hailed a cab and gave the address of the old age home to the driver, a sombre man in his late thirties. After a short while, we arrived at a ramshackle building on the outskirts of the city; at the end of a narrow lane. I told the driver to wait while a security guard ushered me in the manager's office. The yellowed, dilapidated walls of the office were adorned with framed photos of *Mahatma Gandhi* and *Baba Saheb Ambedkar* and also a few group photos of old people engaged in group activities. In one of those frames, they held each other's hand in a chain; under a big tree, smiling at the cameraman and in another, a group of seniors, a few on wheel chairs, raised their hands with the victory sign. I was intrigued. Looking at that frame, I was amused and curious to know what the victory sign was for! Was it for winning a second term at the brink of their lives; or for beating their thankless children by choosing to live in dignity! From the doors of the office which was at the end of a long corridor, I could hear faint voices of men and women. 'Soon, I too will have my voice among them; rejoicing at my victory', I smirked at the thought.

The manager arrived with a dismayed appearance, apologising for making me wait. After settling down in his chair, he offered me a glass of water and said, 'Madam, I do recall that I had promised you a place but I am really sorry. The vacancy was filled since you called last month, we had to.' He apologised. 'But do not worry; I am sure that you would find a place in another old age home where you would be comfortable.' He assured me and wrote an address on a piece of paper. I sighed and with trembling feet got into the waiting cab. I gave the address to the driver who drove to the place not far away from there. It was another nondescript building, an old bungalow with crumbling windows which looked somewhat eerie. I sat and waited in the office. The manager, an old lady entered after a few minutes and sat on her creaking chair. 'Mrs. Shukla, I am really sorry but we might have a vacancy only next year or may be sooner if any inmate leaves or dies.' She was apologetic.

'You will be, for sure, on the top of the waiting list,' she tried to comfort me.

I was perplexed. Back in the cab, I pondered over my options! The driver was concerned by now and could sense my predicament!

'*Maaji*, do not worry, I know the best place for you where you would find a vacancy,' he assured me.

So there was hope! Uncertain of what lay next, I told him to take me there; leaving myself to fate. After a long drive in the city traffic, we reached another building which was flanked by a garden and a big banyan tree. I beamed. The place looked serene and peaceful. I got down and entered the administrator's office with a pounding heart! This was probably my last hope.

A burly lady was seated on the manager's chair, knitting a sweater. She smiled at me as I entered and asked me why I had come. I placed my papers on the scratched table top and narrated how I was turned down by two old age homes; and that I had very high hopes of finding a place in her sanatorium! She smiled with a surprised look on her face, 'Mrs Shukla, I am really sorry but probably you did not notice that sign board at the entrance! This is not an old age Home but an orphanage! You are in a wrong place!'

My heart sank. I murmured an apology and got up.

'Wait, we are looking for a resident warden and if you are ok with it, we may consider hiring you' she said while turning through pages of my resume.

Suddenly I had a renewed hope with this new prospect.

'See, we have very young kids abandoned by their families. They need love and affection of an elderly person like you. I can see that you are a mother and educated too, so I think you could fit in', the manager said.

'Please allow me to show you around before you take the call Mrs. Shukla,' she got up from her chair and escorted me through the rear door of the office which opened into a big crèche. And there they were! Little bundles of joy; carefree and smiling young children full of life, playing, chirping and laughing! Some of them stopped to look at us and smiled at their affectionate warden. The big room reverberated with shrieks and laughter and thumping sounds of tiny feet; clueless of their past and careless about the future!

And then my heartbeats stopped for a moment. There he was, among them, a chubby boy, barely four years old, standing in the far corner of the crèche. He had stopped playing and was resting on his little cricket bat, looking at us with his mischievous eyes, ignoring other kids who coaxed him to resume the play!

I was frozen, and so were my tears! With opaque eyes, I saw my Amit there, the same curly tufts of silken hair hanging on his forehead, those cute dimples in the pink cheeks and that unimpeachable smile! Memories of Amit's childhood and sight of the little boy made me heady. The manager was saying something, but her words were floating around me, my ears numb with a strange sensation!

'Mrs Shukla, are you alright?' She was concerned.

I recollected myself and smiled back at the boy who had his gaze fixed on me.

'Ah, that one is Amit, the naughtiest lad here,' the manager said, pointing to him.

My heart missed a beat again!

'Amit?' I whispered.

'We found him on our steps three years back, when he was barely a year old. So far, no one has come to claim him, what a pity!' she said sadly.

I was in a daze, my thoughts fogged by my emotions and my heart pounding in my chest. By coincidence, life had thrown another chance to me; to give love without expecting to get back where there won't be any contrition or pain of deceit; just pure joy of giving love!

Back in her office, she ordered tea.

I looked at the door to the crèche and saw that innocent smile again. He had followed us to the office and was standing in the doorway; raising his bat high in the air as if urging me to accept the job offer!

So Mrs. Shukla, if you are okay with the terms, you can begin from today itself,' the manager looked at me. I could barely hear her words. I was under some sort of charm, intrigued and drowned in swirls of emotions which I was not able to fathom! By this time, the little lad tottered across the room and clutched the edge of my *saree* with his tiny fingers and looked me in my eyes.

I took him on my bosom and whispered in his tiny ears: 'Yes, let's begin afresh my love!'

* *

SWEET RICE DUMPLINGS

A friend is for ever, let the tide of time and obscurities of life come back and replenish it.

The farmlands burned in the ravaging sun of mid-June; scorching the earth bone dry. The endless tracts of barren lands looked ugly with brittle and half burnt stubs left from the last harvest, waiting to be pulled and ploughed for the new crops. The wind, bereft of moisture blew hot and light and ravaged the earth with unforgiving ferocity.

We were hiding behind a small haystack to escape from the harsh glare of the afternoon sun and chatted. I was with Shibu, the mango harvester's son who was plucking semi ripened mangoes in our orchard not far away where we huddled. Shibu had sneaked past her mother's eyes to meet me in the orchard a few yards away from their hut. We could hear her frantic calls to Shibu who would giggle every time when his worried mother shouted from the other end of the farm.

We were on annual vacation in our village Rudrapur, where we had our ancestral home and mango orchards. I eagerly looked forward to this vacation every year, all the more so because it was my only chance in a year to meet Shibu. He was of almost my age, a tad taller than me, and had dark curly hair on a malnourished head.

Shibu was all ears to my vivid tales of hostel life and the big cities and listened wide eyed. Suddenly a squall of dust startled us. The wind had a hint of chill and dankness. We looked at with awe as a tiny hurricane of dust and dried grass danced and passed away not far from where we sat. A moment later, the skies thundered which had taken a darker hew and looked like a bowl of water with a drop of black ink in it. Suddenly I felt the cool touch of a droplet from the skies on my forehead. The first burst of monsoon rains kissed the sun baked soils and evaporated almost instantly, filling the air with the scent of earth and withered wood. A loud welcome shriek came from the men working in the orchards where my cousins had gathered to supervise the harvesting. I held Shibu's hand and dragged him to the canopy of a big tree and resumed my tales about Bombay, my army school and the life in hostel. He listened with awe, trying to visualize a world he had no idea about, much beyond his imagination; asking questions about fighter jets and the naval ships I had visited with my father.

'So you would also become a commander in navy, like your father?' He asked me.

'No, I want to be a fighter pilot, and what about you?' I looked at him.

Shibu was unsure. After a brief silence, he lowered his eyes and said, 'I do not know, Baba told me that he would send me to the college in the city when I grow up.'

Next day, I was back in the orchard where Shibu was waiting for me with a basket of freshly picked ripe mangoes, while his father and other men packed mangoes in wooden boxes. The harvesting was over and so was my vacation. Next morning, we would go back to Patna to fly to Mumbai; and a week later, I would be back in my naval school hostel. The thought saddened me because I won't be seeing Shibu until next year.

'I brought this for you,' I took out a toy from my pocket, a model fighter plane my father had gifted me and offered him. Shibu's face beamed with awe and excitement. 'So you would fly a plane like this?' There was a sudden spark in his eyes which died the next moment.

'Yes, I would, even you too can but you have to get trained first and selected for the Air Force,' I boasted.

Shibu caressed the model plane gently and carefully slid it in his pocket. 'Would you come next harvesting season?' He asked me after a brief silence. I could see that he was a little morose and unsettled. 'Yes, I would,' I promised and ran to the orchard to join my cousins who were preparing to leave. They looked at me and Shibu with scorn and laughed. I could not understand then why they did not like me hanging out with him. I had noticed that they kept him at a distance and barely spoke to him, except while giving commands. Even Shibu was not comfortable in their presence and avoided to speak to them unless spoken to.

It was the last evening of our vacation and all of our relatives had gathered in our ancestral home to bid farewell to my family. A big feast was arranged for the occasion. Servants were busy preparing food platters and sweets for the dinner while the men and women gathered around *Dadda* (my grandfather) who sat in his carved arm chair with his *hukka*. He was the *Zamindar* in the village, a big and resourceful man with a towering personality.

'A boy has come to meet you,' one of my uncles called me from the veranda, summoning me outside.

It was Shibu, standing at the landing of the stairs leading to the patio! He smiled at me awkwardly, scared and overwhelmed by the opulent house.

'I came with Baba, he had to bring the mango boxes for you to take to Mumbai,' he said, sheepishly. I ran to him and held his hand, almost dragging him up to the Patio.

'Do you like Peethas (sweet rice dumplings, a kind of home made sweet, popular in Bihar)?' I asked him excitedly. Before he could say yes, I ran to the kitchen and looked around. I found a bowl of hot and fresh sweet rice dumplings, my favourite dessert, on the kitchen slab, ready to be served. I grabbed the bowl and sneaked my way outside to Shibu who was looking at the massive house and its interiors with awe.

'Let's have these, my favourite! My mother makes the best of sweet dumplings you have ever eaten' I said and stuffed one in his mouth.

'These are my favourite too,' Shibu was ecstatic, savouring the divine taste of his dream dessert. He picked up the bowl and offered me in return. I smiled at him and gestured him to feed me with his hand.

'Ravi, what are you doing?' The harsh voice of *Dadda* startled us. He stood in the doorway with a stern face, looking at us. Before I could move or say anything, Shibu jumped from the patio and ran away like a terrified hen, dropping the bowl of dumplings on the floor. I tried to call him back but he disappeared in no time.

'We were eating dumplings,' I mumbled meekly to Dadda, trying to fathom my wrongdoing.

Dadda held my shoulders and told me gently, 'Ravi, do you know his caste? you must not eat with him.'

'What is caste *Dadda*?' I was not sure what he was talking about. I protested, 'He is my best friend and we are in the same grades too. *Dadda*, why we cannot eat together?' He smiled and escorted me inside.

That was my last summer vacation in the village. That was also the last time I met Shibu. Early next year we had to move to Cochin for my father's new assignment. A month later, he was stationed in Colombo as part of the Indian peacekeeping force. I was sent to the Naval school in Trivandrum and from there to London for my graduation and aviation pilot training. After coming back to India, I had joined Air force as a combat pilot which was my dream job! Memories of Rudrapur, the mango orchards and the little Shibu slowly faded away amidst the vast expanse of time and its distractions.

Early May, 1999. Western Air Command Post.

The Officers' mess was crowded and noisy as usual on a Friday evening when I entered after completing my sorties. A live band was on the stage playing 'Try to remember' by Harry Belafonte. The air was thick with smoke and alcohol fumes riding on the notes of music. Some of the other pilots of my squadron were sitting on the high chairs at the bar, drinking and cracking jokes. I grabbed a beer and joined them who were singing along the band,

> *'Try to remember the kind of September,*
> *When you were young and callow fellow,*
> *Try to remember and if you remember,*
> *Then follow,*
> *Follow........'*

'Who is this new guy here?' I pointed to a lanky dark young man in *mufti* sitting alone at a table with a bottle of coke. He wore a thin moustache on his hardened face and was humming and smiling at the singer on the stage. I put my beer down and reached to him.

'Hello, I am Squadron leader Ravindra Prakash,' I smiled and extended my hand.

He got up and greeted me. His palm was cold with the chill of his drink.

'Flight Lieutenant Shivram on transfer from the Eastern command Sir. I joined this morning only.' His voice had a heavy modulation and warmth which compensated for the cold hand shake.

'So you joined the base just today! Welcome my dear, be comfortable and by the way, if you need anything, please let me know. Got a place to live?' I asked him.

'No Sir, I am in the bachelors' quarters, no family yet' he smiled back at me.

'Then why do not we meet at dinner at my place tomorrow evening, if you are not busy?"

He beamed and nodded. Turning down a personal invitation by a senior is considered an insult in armed forces.

'Be there at eight' I jotted down my address on a piece of paper and pushed it in his palm. He bowed his head in gratitude, accepting the invitation and sat down in his chair as I returned to my friends at the bar. I quickly finished my beer and left for home where Ma was waiting for me. At the dinner table, I told her about the new pilot and my invite for the dinner.

Shivram arrived next evening with a bouquet of flowers in his hands. After a warm handshake, I introduced him to Ma. He bowed down and touched Ma's feet. I offered him a whiskey as we settled down on the dining table.

'No thanks, I do not drink' he refused politely and took a glass of soft drink.

So which part of country you are from?' I asked him.

'I am from a remote village in Bihar, and you?' he looked at me with curiosity, sipping his coke.

'We too are from Bihar but never really stayed there. Dad was in navy and so we were on the move all the times,' I told him while Ma ignored his protests and put another paratha on his plate.

'Bihar?' he was curious.

'Come on, how does it matter anyway!' I shrugged him, pointing to the sky, drawing a flight path with my hand in the air, 'Up there, you do not have any state, religion or caste! You fly, live and die for the motherland and nothing else matters,' I said my favourite punch line with theatrical melodrama and laughed aloud.

During the dinner we talked about life in the base and the growing tension on the northern borders. I could see that he was slightly unsettled, probably homesick. This was not surprising as new pilots had very gruelling routine and leaves were seldom granted.

We finished our dinner and settled on the sofa, waiting for the dessert.

Ma came out of the kitchen with a bowl, full of steaming sweet rice dumplings. I was disappointed.

'Ma, you know I do not like dumplings and I am not sure about Shivram as well. Can we have some ice cream instead?' I fussed like a child.

'I know, but they are for your friend and not for you, isn't it so?' She chided me affectionately and offered the bowl to Shivram.

Shivram's dark eyes were fixed on those dumplings. With a playful grin, I pointed my finger to him and said 'Ma, see, he too does not like them.' I dared him.

'I had them only once, in my childhood, and never after that,' Shivram whispered; his gaze still fixed on the dumplings.

'What a coincidence! Even I stopped eating them, long back when I was very young.' I laughed aloud and suddenly stopped in my tracks.

Those dumplings were rustling up memories and forgotten images withered by the passage of time. I leaned forward and looked at him keenly, trying to rekindle those reminiscences faded long back but they were hazy, as if hidden behind an opaque screen.

'Rudrapur?' Shivram whispered.

I was almost on the edge of the sofa, my fingers clutching the armrest. Suddenly the fog lifted and I could see my little rendezvous with Shibu in the orchard, his terrified face and the dumplings rolling on the dusty floor of the patio. With trembling fingers, he took a small model plane from his pocket and placed it on the coffee table gently. The paint on the toy had faded at places and the metal had some chinks but I recognised it instantly.

'I never ate sweet dumplings since then,' he mumbled, staring at the bowl.

'Even I,' my voice shook as I reached to hug him. I picked up the bowl and stuffed a dumpling in his mouth.

* *

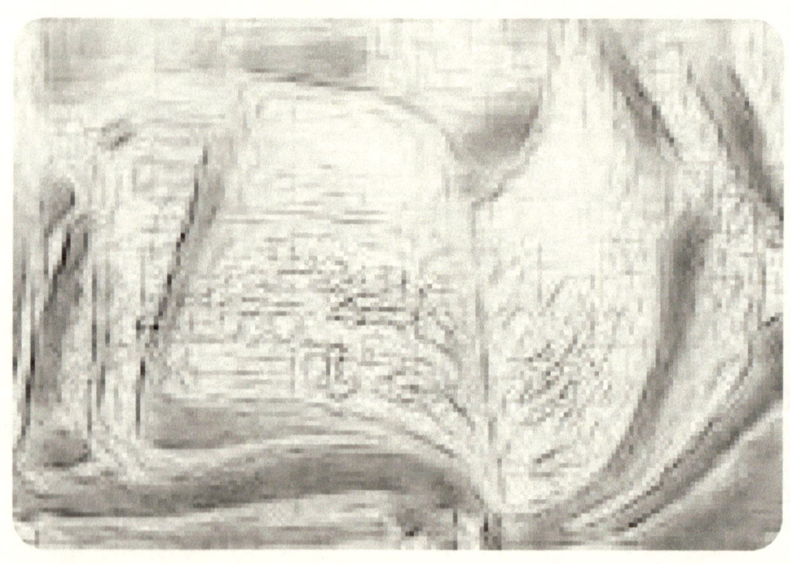

A FATHER'S DIARY

Are not your longings and dreams above mine? Don't I see my bliss in your happiness? If life cannot prove it, let the death do.

Lying on his rug on the coarse floor of his shanty, Manu looked up at the blue tarpaulin roof above him. The tattered sheet was gently pulsating in the morning breeze with a hushed vibration, like wings of a humming bird. Razor sharp slivers of sunlight seeping in through the holes in the sheet made queer patterns on the tin walls and gravelled floor of the shabby room. He struggled to open his groggy eyes and sat on the rug under him and looked aimlessly in the poorly lit room. He got up and painstakingly tottered to the flimsy door of the tenement and out to the littered compound of the slum. The railway tracks a few yards away looked like a giant anaconda, running endlessly to the west, merging with the horizon at the far end. Some people from the slum around him were still asleep on rusted camp cots amid mounds of stinking garbage. A few stray dogs were digging in the heaps of trash silently lest they be noticed and shooed away. Alarmed by Manu's footsteps, they scattered. The slum around him was silent, barring the sound of coughing from a shanty. He strolled farther to have a look at the rickety building of the railway station a few hundred yards away where the tracks took a turn. The lone platform was barren as the first train would stop only after a couple of hours later.

Manu returned to the hut and sat on the cold gravelled floor which hurt. In a corner of the shack, a bright shining red bicycle rested against the wall, the cellophane wrapping from the showroom still intact on it. It looked out of place in the filthy and disarranged surrounding. A big jute sack filled with trash he had collected the day before, stood in another corner, ready to be sorted and sold to the one eyed scrap dealer in the town. He grimaced at the deceit of the shrewd man who would always cheat him and refuge to pay fair price for his toiling. With closed eyes, he clenched his fists and vowed to take revenge on him when he would grow as tall as his father. The days when he would pick trash along with his father Laxman, they commanded better price. Laxman was not easy to be fooled as he bargained hard with the dealer. Together, they would often made good money enough to buy rice and vegetables for the day and even save some. On those days, Laxman would buy a bottle of arrack and boiled peas for himself and candies for Manu. After finishing the arrack, he would be totally whooshed, and come out of the hut; swaying, throwing his hairy arms in the air and shouting incoherently till Manu or his mother dragged him back indoors. There he would lie on the floor, spread eagled, mumbling curses and then sleep; snoring loudly, which kept Manu and his mother awake through the night.

Manu sighed and got up, his tiny bones aching in his slender frame. He was frail and tired with the hard work and his back hurt. Even while off work, he could feel the load of the heavy sack on his small back, like that of a saddle on a pony. He was hungry. Rummaging through the tin boxes on the shelf, he found a half emptied pack of biscuits he had salvaged from a garbage bag. Although crumbled, they were not yet soggy. He munched on them, relishing the crunch of chocolate chips in the cookies, wondering who could throw those fresh cookies in trash! After emptying the pack, he poured some water in a steel glass from the earthen pot in the corner and drank feverishly. Holding the stained glass in his palm which his father drank from, he looked at it and shuddered with the memory of the night which had toppled his life.

A week back, Manu had hit upon a small fortune while sorting trash from the garbage bins in a colony of rich people in the town. He had found a ring, probably thrown accidently in the trash. He took it to his father who examined it closely and confirmed that it was gold. Hiding the ring under clothes, they left the place hurriedly and went to a pawn shop at the far end of the town. The shop owner looked at them with contempt.

'You guys stole it, did not you?' He asked with scorn.

They kept silence.

The shop owner handed them a small wad of currency notes.

'No one would give you more than this. I don't want to see you here again, do not talk about it and; and yes, never come back,' he growled and shooed them away.

They huddled in a lonely corner at the far end of the deserted road and counted the money.

'It is only three thousand, the ring was worth ten thousand, for sure. The scoundrel has cheated us', Laxman lamented, hiding the money under his vest.

Laxman's eyes shone with the rekindled hope, the hope he had lost for years in the dark alleys filled with filth and garbage: his last wish of seeing his father before he died. Now wiith this windfall, he could plan their travel to his birthplace, to meet his father. His thoughts were meandering decades back to his childhood, his father's face fading from his memories and his step mother's torments. After all these years, he could still feel the chill of his tears rolling on his cheeks and his cries for his dream which had shattered; like glass pebbles crushed under a stone pestle; it's fragments haunting him for decades; from the day he had left his home and Babuji. He lived with those memories and his broken dream every single day and night, whether awake or asleep.

Childhood dreams are probably the strongest memories; for however long those sleep, would swing back like a dried sapling coming back to life with touch of water in its roots. We sleep, see dreams and forget them the next day, but dreams seen with open eyes, particularly those blossoming out of a loss or sorrow never die; harnessing their strength from our trauma and fixity of tragedy. The fuel of desolation and remorse keep them alive and burning like the perpetual fire in temples burning amidst turbulent gushes of wind.

Manu's eyes sparkled with hope. He had, for long, eyed a red bicycle in a shop in the city but dared not ask Laxman. Somehow he gathered his courage and asked him feebly, 'Baba, can we buy a bicycle, on my Birthday?'

Laxman froze, the dark reminiscence of his own childhood coming back to life and hitting him; like a stone hits an expanse of still waters, creating ripples. Still wrapped in his memories, he squeezed the currency notes in his fist and looked at him lovingly. 'Sure, we would also buy your books and some good pens as well.' He mumbled. His dream had shattered but another one was blooming. He felt ecstatic, his tragic past and the power of doing the undoable swept over him with pride of conquering the past and sense of fruition swelling in his chest.

His dreams and wishes could wait!

Manu could not believe his luck! He exclaimed with joy and ran to his mother to tell her the news.

That year, Manu's birthday was a great day of jubilation for the family. All of them went to the market with the booty. After buying the bicycle, Laxman bought a cake, a saree for his wife and a pair of shorts and some books for Manu with the money left. And not to forget, he bought a bottle of the flavoured 'English liquor' for himself which he had fancied for long, and some chicken for dinner. Then they walked back home; an ecstatic Manu riding his new bike.

That evening was of celebration. Manu's mother cooked the chicken and rice while Laxman merrily gulped the arrack from the steel glass, thanking Gods for the windfall. A jubilant Manu rode on the bicycle, paddling in circles around the slum with a bunch of envious children in tow. When the dinner was ready, Rani, Manu's mother called him in and the family sat on the floor and ate with much relish. Laxman looked at the stars through the door as if thanking them and then at his wife who was battered with poverty and fatigue of their cruel life. Holding the bottle of liquor in one hand he held her arm and mumbled words laced with alcohol, 'Rani, I love you, I promise that I will fulfil all your dreams, won't I? I wish you be my wife in my next seven lives' He laughed aloud. Then he awkwardly hugged Manu, struggling to remain on his feet. Totally inebriated, he limped out of the hut with the bottle of booze in his hand to the railway tracks to relieve himself while Rani looked at him in disgust.

'Seven lives he said? Huh! Seven more lives with you in hell! Is this was not enough! Never!' She blurted at him, collecting the soiled utensils.

The shrill whistle of the train engine startled them.

'Baba', Manu shouted and ran to his father out of the hut who was on the tracks to relieve himself, swaying with the bottle in his clutch. It was pitch dark outside save for the beam of the train engine which hurtled towards Laxman with great speed. The massive locomotive whistled again. Probably the motorman had spotted him on the tracks and was whistling to alert him. But Laxman was not hearing, his senses being opaque by the toxic booze. A few feet away from him, Manu froze in terror. With his heart thumping in his chest, he yelled at his father who swayed on the tracks like a scare crow wobbling in a paddy field. Manu ran to him and caught hold of his sleeve and tried to drag him away from the tracks but Laxman stood firm amidst the stone pebbles between the tracks; daring the blinding yellow beam of the locomotive which was now very close. The harsh light and the shrill noise of the hooter numbed Manu and he fell backwards. The next moment he felt the arms of his mother grabbing his shoulders, dragging him away from the rails. She tripped over him but stretched her arms to get hold of Laxman while pushing Manu away from the tracks. In that split second of perplexity and panic, Laxman dragged Rani towards himself and both of them fell on the tracks. The next thing Manu remembered before passing out was the shrill screeching sound of the metal brakes and heart wrenching cry of her mother.

Next morning, the neighbours arranged the funeral of his parents. Manu sat silently, dazed, crying and watching the pyres; oblivious of people around him. Those flames were taking his world; his mother away from him. He was numb, feeling nothing; no pain or remorse, no memories but just a plain inexplicable void which had sucked all what he felt or remembered about them. Although he wept, there were no tears in his eyes; they had dried in the ocean of shock and trauma which had drowned his little world.

Once the smoke from the pyres died, his neighbours brought him back to his shanty and comforted him. Beaten by the devastating events of the last night, he fell asleep, only to wake up after a while, hallucinating, her mother's face swivelling in the acrid curls of black smoke from her pyre, stretching her arms to him and disappearing the next moment as the gush of wind tore into the fumes.

In his nightmares of sorrow and loss, which continued for weeks; he could never see his father, his thoughts wandering to the terrifying sound of the train, and to his mother in the death embrace of Laxman and her heart tearing cries for help. He shuddered. A tsunami of hate for his father was rising in his heart who was his bête noire; it was he who had crushed him under his cruelty and scolding and snatched his mother, the only person in world he adored, in whose lap his universe began and ended; whose bosom his tormented heart found solace in. His raze and anger for his father grew as he recalled his harsh words and unending chidings. 'Do not you want to achieve something in life? Do you think you ever become rich by picking this filth! I toil day and night so that you can become a rich man one day like those Sahibs living in bungalows, do not you want that?' He would shout at him.

He hated him for everything, for he dragged him to work and the night school after his bone braking shift of rag picking. Laxman would sit outside the school, waiting for him, lest he bunked his periods. Once the classes were over, Manu would run home; to the waiting embrace of his mother. She would never be harsh to him and always shielded him from her husband's bouts of frustration and rage. Her embrace was his assuagement from the cruel universe of theirs where his childhood was buried under the heaps of stink and garbage!

From beneath his blackened pillow, he took out a wooden photo frame for hundredth time since that fateful night and looked at the faded sketch which he had drawn in the evening school. It was of a woman clad in a red saree, smiling and holding a tiny finger of a child. The glass of the discoloured frame had cracks but he could clearly see her mother. There was his father too in the drawing but he had folded the paper so that he won't see him in the frame; he wanted it that way! Looking at the sketch, he hated him more than ever for he was the one who had snatched his mother from him. He would often wake up, sweating and sobbing when he saw her in his dreams, clad in a white saree like an angel, smiling at him and stretching her arms to embrace him. Laxman was never in his dreams, nor in his cries, not even in his tender sub conscious; his detestation for him was too strong to see him even in his imaginations.

It was more than a month since they were gone. The contribution of food from the neighbours had dried up but he had little courage left for work or to go to the evening school he hated. Somehow he gathered his strength and dragged the heavy sack to the door for the long haul to the scrap dealer. A battered small tin box on the top shelf of the wall rack caught his eyes. It was Laxman's box which he would keep locked and not allow him or even his mother to open. He put the sack on the ground and looked around for something to break the lock and found a small knife. The pad lock broke with a click. Inside the box were some tattered books, an old wallet with some coins and a photo of Goddess Durga. With curious eyes, he searched deeper and found a small, battered notebook with a half torn cover hidden under the clothes. He opened the notebook and instantly recognised his father's handwriting. Manu began shuffling the pages which had yellowed and become brittle with age. He squatted on the floor and began reading.

(17 Aug,1968)

It seems that one wants me. Nayi ma has some spell on Babuji since the day he brought her home. I know he loves me and cares for me but has no guts to dare the woman he has married. She won't stop torturing me. Last night she beat me very badly and even broke my finger. What was my fault! She became furious at me for I asked Babuji to buy me a bicycle on my birthday next week. Babuji had said yes but she won't let him to. I would have been happy with even an old one! Whom should I go and cry to!

(23 Aug)

Today was my birthday. Babuji did not buy the bicycle, though he wanted to. When I asked him, nayi ma beat me and threw the cake on the floor Babuji had brought. I saw tears in Babuji's eyes. He is helpless and so am I. In the night, I left home while everyone was asleep. But one day I will come back for sure to see Babuji and take him away from this woman; I promise.

I am writing this in a train, far away from home. I do not know where I am going, but any place would be much better than that house. I have left behind everything. The only thing I want is to see Babuji before I die, this is my only wish.

(No date, 1985)

Writing my diary after so many years. In fact there was not much to write. Last year I married Rani. She is from this slum only, an orphan. Life is tough but I believe in God, He would sure be pleased someday.

(11 Jan, 1986.)

Looks like God has finally heard my prayers. Rani is pregnant. Now we will be three of us. Have to work harder to earn more.

(7 October, 1987)

Our star is borne. It is a boy. Rani wanted a girl but I had always prayed for a boy. Have even thought his name. We will call him Manu. He Looks exactly like me! Durga Ma, a million thanks to you. I have requested Kishan's mother from the next hut to care for them when I go for work.

(7 Octber, 88)

Today is Manu's first birthday. He is crawling all ove the place and giggles when I lift him up. We had saved some money for the feast on his first Birthday. I wish Babuji sees him. The day I have enough money, I will take all of us to meet him. It cannot say how happy he would be when he sees Rani and his grandson!

(No date)

Have not written my diary for a while. Manu is now more than 5 years old. Last month I put him in the Government school. He would study and become a big man and have servants like those sahibs in the town. I am not sure if I live to see that, but I swear, he would not suffer like I did. Would do anything to see that.

Some of the pages were torn and soiled. A few pages had some accounts and addresses written over periods of time.

With trembling fingers, Manu shuffled the pages to reach the last written page.

(no date)

Today God finally listened to our prayers. We found some money. At first I thought of taking all of us to Babuji to fulfil my last wish. This was my dream. I had planned it all; even buying new clothes for him and bringing him here to live with us. He would take Manu to school, play with him and even teach him! And this time I will not be helpless.

He had continued writing on the next page.

Nature has its strange ways! While I planned all this, Manu said that he wanted a bicycle on his birthday.

When he asked this, everything that happened on my birthday came alive before me! It was that day, when I had asked for a bicycle from Babuji. Nai Ma shouted at us. She even thrashed me and hurled the chocolate cake on the floor. I had cried and fled home on that day, my birthday!

It was difficult to decide but how could I refuse Manu? What happened with me, must not happen with him. His wish is above mine, so let it be. We will buy his bicycle. I will wait till Gods become happy again, then we would go to see Babuji. Are not his dreams mine as well?, Aren't those?

(7 September, 2001)

We all went to the cycle shop today. Manu liked a red bicycle. It is a bit expensive but he wanted only that one, so be it. He is so happy. What else I want! The other day he did not speak to me because I had shouted at him. Well, I was right. He wanted to play in the evening instead of attending his classes. He has to study or else he would remain a rag picker like me for the rest of his life. I know he does not like me, as I am strict to him. He loves his mother more but I have to be tough on him or else he would be spoiled, so be it.

Manu closed the diary and clenched it against his chest. Tears rolled down his cheeks when he picked up the photo frame and unfolded the paper to see the faded sketch of his father. His stare fixed on the drawing, he wept for him for the first time!

* *

LOVE HAS NO BOUNDARIES

True lovers, break all the shackles to be with someone you adore, for you won't find a cause for living as virtuous as that.

Many centuries ago, when travellers and traders walked through perilous terrains; braving elements and bandits, a handsome crown prince, who was young in heart and brave in his demeanours; ventured out of his empire into the jungle with a small entourage. After days of trekking and hunting in treacherous wilds, their convoy was attacked by bandits who ambushed them and killed all his men; leaving him wounded. After sometime, when they were gone, he gathered his strength and dragged himself to the edge of the forest where he saw a building standing amidst nowhere. He cautiously approached the place whose doors were open and welcoming and found that it was an inn, a safe shelter for the tired travellers. The weary prince, who was gravely injured and had shed a large amount of blood, fell at the door of the inn and passed out.

After many days when he opened his eyes, he saw many worried faces hovering over him; examining his wounds and nursing him. Among those was an imposing man with a long beard in a white gown who asked him softly, ' How do you feel my son? Do your wounds still hurt!'

Overwhelmed with gratitude and thankfulness, the prince nodded and smiled, although he was still very weak and could not move. Behind that man of authority, stood a stunningly beautiful girl. Her looks were feline ; her long hairs like fine strands of gold and hazel eyes with sparks of a million stars. She was looking at him with perturbation and concern.

'You are fortunate to survive in the hands of those barbarians, but now you are safe in this shelter. I am owner of this inn and also the chieftain of my clan. Who are you and where you came from?' The man in the white gown asked with much adoration.

The prince; battered by his injuries, tried to say some words which were not coherent and audible as he was too feeble.

'Never mind, you first regain your strength and we will talk then. My men and my daughter Syra would take care of you;' He said, looking fondly at the girl who smiled at him; filling the room with brilliance of a thousand suns.

In a few days, he regained his vigour by the untiring efforts of the physicians and the girl who always remained at his side whenever he opened his eyes. By this time, the chieftain and the other men and women in the inn knew who he was and were even more respectful and attendant to him. As time went by while he recuperated under the fond care of Syra, he was struck and smitten by her grace and charm, and fell in love with her whom he owed his life to.

The reverberations of the love stricken heart of the prince had aroused similar feelings in Syra's heart. He had expressed his feelings to Syra who had not met a man as handsome and charismatic as him. She too was struck by the charm of the handsome prince who was the man of her dreams; her Godsend destiny! But she was wary of her father and the rules of their clan which did not permit anyone; not even the chieftain's daughter to marry outside their clan! But by this time her heart was filled with nothing but endearments for him and did not want to lose him! One day, while they were alone in his room, she held his palm and whispered, 'My father won't give my hand to anyone outside the clan, not even to a prince! The only way for us to be together is elopement.'

The prince who was firm in his resolve to get her; thought over it and said, 'My enlightened father has taught me among many things; that I must not deceive someone who obliges me, not for any virtue or wealth, however dear it might be and also that I must return a favour multi fold, even with my life, if it demands so. I have also learnt from him that under any circumstances, I must not break a person's trust, especially of the one who saves my life and entrust his dearest thing to me,! Your noble father has saved my life and entrusted you to nurse me while I was fighting for my life. How can I elope with you! How can I thrust the dagger of deceit in the kind heart of a man who stitched my wounds and prayed for my life!'

'I will beg him, even kneel before him if it takes to that. I am sure that he would melt down and accept my prayer.' The prince said.

So the next morning, when her father came to his bedside to ask his wellbeing, the prince sat on his bed and greeted him and pleaded with lowered eyes in the most submissive and unassertive voice, 'You are my saviour for which I am indebted to you for my life! But the favour I am going to ask now is way more precious to me and you than my life which you saved! I want to marry your daughter and make her the queen of my empire. I promise you with my life that I will give her my love and happiness not less than you have!'

The chieftain's eyes had tears of pain; for he, over last few days; had seen the sparks of cheer and torment in his dear daughter's eyes and had fathomed her feelings for the prince. He looked at her daughter and said in a voice laced with despair, 'My prince, I won't find a better match for my girl even beyond the expanse of the seven seas, but the laws of my lands do not permit this; as you know.' He bowed and left the grieving prince with a heavy heart. Once in his court, he called his Ministers and asked for a solution.

After long deliberations, the Minister-in-chief got up from his seat and whispered in the ears of the chieftain who smiled and nodded in agreement.

The Chieftain immediately went to the heartbroken prince and said, 'My advisors have suggested a solution. If you agree to renounce your clan and take oath of allegiance to our Gods to be my heir to the throne, we can permit this alliance.'

The prince was taken aback. Aghast and hurt; he looked at him and said, 'This is not possible! How can I subjugate my Gods and my father for the sake of my lust! I can give any sacrifice; even renounce my crown for your daughter but what you ask is sacrilege!'

The chieftain shook his head in dismay and said, 'In that case my Prince, you may proceed to your kingdom whenever you wish to; with our full honours and humble gifts for your noble father!'

The innkeeper bowed and left. Thereafter he went to his daughter and said, 'My dear child, not a single day in my life has passed when I have not prayed for you and your happiness; or not sought my bliss in your beautiful eyes. My heart weeps when I see tears in them. But I am tied with the limitations of our traditions. However, my Ministers have opined that if you promise to discard this tribe and recant our Gods, I would give my consent to the prince's proposal.'

Syra looked at her father lovingly for she knew that if she agrees to that; it would break her father's heart whose world revolved around her. She hugged him in embrace and said, 'My dear father, no treasure in this world or beyond can lure me to break apart from you or renounce my clan. You have given me birth and so I owe you the air I breathe and the blood which runs in my veins! I will not give up your patronage for anything; however precious it may be for the sake of my happiness!'

So the next morning, the forlorn prince left their inn and was escorted to his kingdom where a grand welcome awaited him. To celebrate the safe return of the prince, the king had ordered grand celebrations and feasts all around. But the prince whose heart had shattered a million times, wept for her love; even more so since he knew that she too wept for him and won't live long without him. No one heard their wailings, quashed under the sounds of fireworks and diktats of the cruel society!

The prince grew more abject and disconsolate as the days passed. He remained morose and refused meeting people or venturing out as Syra's memories haunted her even more than ever. He tried to find a way out of the abyss he had fallen into, but more he tried, deeper he sank. He fell sick while his desolate soul wandered in the inn, looking for Syra. The king who was alerted of his condition, came to his palace and sat beside his loving son and said, 'What is on this earth which troubles you my dear son, just name it and I will extinguish it from its face! Or if you desire anything that Gods have created in the universe, I will bring it to your feet to make you smile.' The prince looked at his worried father and told him about the love of his life and that why her stubborn father won't give her hands to him.

The king was enraged! 'How a trifle chieftain can refuse my son who has the most beautiful princesses in the world queued up to wed! I will dispatch my armies to drag him to my court and make him kneel before you and beg you to marry her daughter!

The prince said, 'No father, I will not agree to such alliance which crushes their tradition; and hurt her for she loves her father more than anything in this world! Moreover, I am indebted to him for my life and have vowed not to harm him for he was the one who saved me from my certain death. How can I think of harming or disrespecting him?' He said with resolve.

The king retreated, leaving his son writhing in pain and despair.

It was not before a fortnight when the distraught prince who was at the brink of breaking down, went to his father and said, 'If you want to see me alive, please permit me to go to her tribe and beg for her hand on their terms.'

The perturbed father had no choice but to accept his son's say; his heart broken by the thought of losing his son and heir to his throne.

The prince went alone to the inn where he was given a warm welcome sans the sight of her paramour. After settling down in his room, he was escorted to the court where the chieftain sat with his advisors and Ministers. He came down from his high chair and greeted the prince in a manner befitting him. The prince bowed his head and said, 'I am ready to take your daughter as my wife on your terms, or whatever conditions you put.' The chieftain nodded while the men in the court cheered in joy.

'Let me ask my daughter,' He said and ordered to bring Syra in the courtroom.

She had diminished; haunted by her memories and the void she had slipped into. Her sheen had faded and the sparkles in her hazel eyes had turned to ashes! Caught in the dilemma of losing either her love or the world which she was bound to, her soul was crushed; afterlife now being the only refuse where she could find peace. So when she saw the prince, her teary eyes refused to believe it was him. Haunted by her despair and trauma, she wanted to believe that she was hallucinating in the lap of death! The prince gasped at her sight! He wanted to run to her and rejuvenate her in his embrace, give her the last drop of his blood to reinvigorate her and to bring her back to their lives which were torn apart by cruel sword of separation. Before they could utter a word, the chieftain faced her daughter and said, 'My love, now tell me you want to be with this man; on the conditions I had put!'

'Yes father,' She whispered; her thoughts turned opaque by her desperation; clinging to the last shred of hope to be with the man to whom she had assigned her life.

'And you my dear prince, are you ready to give up all you have, your Gods and your kingdom; to wed my daughter?' He turned to the prince who too nodded in affirmation.

The prince and Syra looked at each other in joy and astonishment; both unaware of the conditions put before each of them. The chieftain rose from his seat and took both of them in his embrace and announced, 'My dear children, my guilty heart cries at the affliction and torment both of you have suffered from. But this was the only way which my wise Ministers had suggested; not to subjugate or humiliate you; but to test the truth and resilience of your love and to see to what stretch you can go to meet the commitments you made to each other! Love has no boundaries, nor its commitments are bound by terms and conditions laid by any mortal on this earth! The grandeur and magnanimity of your true and pious love is proven far above this world and its fragile laws. You two are one now; unbound by any condition or will which are not yours!

Then he ordered preparation for their wedding!

* *

CRIME & KARMA

The wheel of karma stops at reward and damnation; but who rotates the wheel and stops it!

In the pile of mail on my desk, a mutilated envelope with overseas postal stamps caught my eyes. Inside the envelope was the familiar new year greeting card signed 'Sunder and Aditi' in red ink with a smiley drawn below it. The envelope also had a family photograph. Looking at the photograph, a faint smile came on my lips. The man had aged and had wrinkles on his withered face but I could never fail in recognising him. Next to him stood a middle aged fair and slim woman, her head covered with an embroidered scarf with a fair complexioned girl in her early twenties with quaint eyes, smiling to the camera.

For last several years those cards would somehow land on my office desk around this time with the same scribble, at times with a small note with broken words of pleasantries or a photograph. I had never acknowledged them or replied to but they kept on coming on every new year eve, hurdling me 18 years back to Mumbai (then Bombay) when I had my first encounter with Sunder and Aditi.

1992, Bombay

The battered court room was beginning to fill slowly. The huge British era room was cluttered with rickety furniture and dirty bundles of papers wrapped in red muslin, piled all around. The cramped room smelled of mould and brittle and yellowed documents. A tired fan blackened by dust and soot hanged from a wooden beam in the high ceiling; its rusty blades slowly rotating with painful squeaks. The front row of chairs in the courtroom was mostly occupied by clerks and lawyers in their black jackets and robes. Against a windowless wall, a few under trials sat on a backless bench. Stern faced uniformed sentries clutched their fingers and restrained them from getting up. One of the under trials, a middle aged man, shrieked with joy when he saw a family member inside the court. He was promptly rebuked by the sentry. Another morose prisoner tried to look over the shoulders in the crowd, looking for someone he was expecting and grimaced when he found none.

I entered the court room a little before the Magistrate was to take his seat and headed straight to the public prosecutor who was saddled in a chair in the front row. After a brief conversation with him, I backed off, looking for a place to settle down.

Sunder was sitting at the far end in the row with other under trials, next to a sentry in uniform. He wore a crumpled white shirt and a pair of dirty and worn out jeans. His lips were dry and dishevelled hair hung on his shoulders. Alerted by my gaze, he raised his head slightly and looked at me with forlorn eyes. I was intrigued and curious to know what he could have been thinking of me! I was his persecutor; I was the reason he was there, facing trial and most probably a harsh punishment for his crime! I wondered if he still hanged with his thin thread of hope that I could save him, give him a chance to bewail and let him absolve himself of his deeds; set him free to go back to his happy world in his hills and ending that nightmare he was living with!

In my career as a narcotics enforcement officer, I had closely studied many of my subjects- novices, intelligent ones and hardened criminals. A few, especially the 'first timers' repented for their deeds on being caught and showed remorse. Ignorant or having little knowledge of law, very few of this type understood the severity and implication of their crime. Some of them, especially the sombre ones would open up their past lives when coaxed; and seek help in undoing their crime and rehabilitating their souls. The more hardened ones and the 'repeat offenders' would not express their regret, rather not speak at all. They probably thought that the system was not in their favour and they were the victims of unjust environs which were prejudiced; and hence their deeds were consequential and well grounded. Criminals of this type had no qualms about justifying their deeds and asserted that their crime was much lesser than those of the mighty and powerful who escaped the clutches of law. However, I felt that penitence still lurked in deep corners of their hearts too, waiting for more persuasion and concerted effort to scoop it out.

Remorse and conscience of a man are always in conflict; both tainted with and complimenting each other like two sides of a coin, albeit struggling to subjugate the other side. It is just the matter of time and influence when one dominates the other. Both rectitude and deceit get their feed from our emotions and feelings which stay in the same abode inside us- our heart; competing for space and to find grounds!

Sunder was a 'drug mule,' a traveller on hire, who carries narcotics for others in lieu of money. To become a drug mule, one needs very strong motivation, as the consequences of being caught were serious. Most of the time, poverty and instant gratification happen to be the best motivators. The compensation is usually good which includes journey to a 'foreign country' and a fat purse on successful delivery. The lure of quick money often obliterates the risk of being arrested and harsh punishment, even death penalty in some countries.

I had arrested Sunder a couple of days back at the airport while he was attempting to smuggle out heroin. He had stated that he came from a small village in the mountains of Satyavati district in Nepal where he had lived with his wife and a girl child until a day when he was lured by a person who came from Kathmandu and put an offer he could not refuge. The money could change his fate and he was desperate to do anything to take his family out of the squalor and misery.

During the search of his belongings, I had found a family photograph in which his wife, a young petite woman stood between him and a little girl, smiling at each other at the door of their humble home in the mountains.

'They would die without me, there is none in the family except me to feed them. Please have mercy on me sir.' He had wailed when I arrested him and explained the impending doom of trial and punishment, if convicted. As the insurmountable consequences of his act unfolded before him, he became scared and desolate; his eyes telling his repentance and struggle to undo his past and the crime he had committed.

Waiving the photograph in front of his eyes, I snapped, 'You should have thought of them before doing this. You reap what you sow, don't you? Now you must face the consequences. But if you help us nabbing the masterminds who gave you the drug to carry, I will try that you get a lesser term or even consider making you a prosecution wutness,' I tried to lure him into giving more information about the racket. Nonetheless, I was sure that he won't be having any clue about the real plotters. Narcotics trafficking involves multi layered chain of commands from veiled identities and pseudo names and a drug mule stands no chance to find out or identify the masterminds.

I took my eyes off him and waited for the remand proceedings to begin. As the bailiff took his position near the door of the ante room which opened to the wooden dais where the Magistrate sat, the murmur inside the room receded to hushed tones. In a few moments, the bailiff announced the arrival of the Magistrate in a stern voice. The court room had a pin drop silence, except the screeching sound of the battered ceiling fan. No sooner than the Magistrate had settled in his chair behind his huge desk, the bailiff began calling cases by their numbers in his rhetoric voice.

'Sunder Chankhe Tamang versus Union Of India'. The bailiff announced without looking away from his list. Coaxed by the constable, Sunder stood, hands folded, his eyes moving between me and the Magistrate expectantly. After a brief hearing and a lame appeal by the defence counsel, the Magistrate scribbled on his file and announced curtly, 'Fourteen days remand to Judicial custody granted; department to file interim investigation progress report on the next date.' Before Sunder could understand a word of the order, the sentry dragged him out of the court to the waiting Jail van.

To me, it was just another case and another accused. We would complete investigation in a couple of months or so while Sunder would be in custody followed by a sentence! It was an open and shut case; another closed file in the closet and another accused left to rot for next ten years or so among the high prison walls. Sunder's name would soon be relegated to just a case number in the files. My job would be over, in the line of my duties.

Little did I know that the events that would unfold in coming days would realign my surmise of actions and their reverberations, my beliefs on karma; change the way I reckoned my deeds and their prevalence over others' lives and shake my preconceived notion of actions and their consequences. I had no inkling of the storm which was lurking to hit Sunder and my understanding of karma, crime and punishment.

A week later, I visited him in the jail to record his further statement. It was a routine process. Sunder was waiting in the Jailor's room when I arrived. He had shrunk; standing in a dejected posture in a corner of the bare room which had only a table and couple of chairs. His eyes were hollowed and his head hung on his shoulders. I was not surprised. I had seen how life in jails broke even hardened criminals, especially the first timers or the ones who were repentant of their wrongdoings! Solitude, fear of a new and hostile place and the horrendous life in confinement battered them and sucked the sap of their souls.

I sat on the chair and gestured him to sit across the table to scribe his statement. He sat, his face hung on his chest in dejection. I could see that he was crying silently, wiping his tears. For a few minutes, he remained silent, not answering my questions. Then suddenly, he squeezed my palm and began weeping bitterly. I was a bit unnerved, though not surprised, and freed my hands gently. 'Are you alright? Did anyone trouble you here?' I asked with concern.

He cried inconsolably, trying to speak but the words were muffled by his sobs.

'Sir, please help me, I have no one else here to help me out. Please save my wife Sir.' He spoke, composing himself.

I was taken aback. 'What about your wife; what happened to her?' I had not expected this.

In a voice laced with desperation and broken by sobs, he said, 'Sir, when I came here, I received a letter from her saying that she was on her way to Bombay to see me and would reach the day before yesterday. She was supposed to call my lawyer but he told me this morning that he had not heard from her so far.

'Well, she must have changed the plan?' I said.

'No, last night, an inmate was brought here from a red light area whom I met in the courtyard. He told me that a Nepali woman was kidnapped from Bombay Central station a couple of days back and taken to some brothel in Kamathipura. When I showed him my wife's photograph, he confirmed that he had seen her and was sure that it was her. Sir, He confirmed that it was Aditi, he cannot be wrong,' Sunder broke down, clutching my hands even harder and crying inconsolably.

'For God's sake, help me sir, I will never do anything wrong again in my life. I swear on her and my daughter. I have ruined my family.' He sobbed, pulling his hair, tears of desperation rolling down his cheeks.

'You had told me that you reap what you sow, but look at me Sir, why am I reaping a hundred times of what I sowed! She did nothing wrong but then why God is punishing her for my deeds!' He got up from his chair and fell on my feet, pleading and crying, rubbing his forehead on my shoes!

I was stunned by the shockwaves of his pain and remorse, hitting hard in my face! I did want him to face the consequences of his crime; but would the consequences go so far and wide? Was his wife destined to face the punishment for his deeds, and if so, which hypothesis of universe or law of religion says it; and who or what ould decide the quantum of that punishment and why?

I had no answers!

My concern had ignited a tiny sparkle of hope in his swollen eyes. With trembling fingers, he pushed a photograph in my palms, 'Sir, hang me for what I did, but why she should be punished for my crime, please do something, save her please' he pleaded.

I came back home, questions pounding my conscience, my thoughts struggling to find a ground where I could see actions and their emanation more clearly. Were Sunder's karma behind the impending doom of his wife? And if yes, how and why? Do our karma have ramifications more than what is visible, like an iron ball hitting a concrete wall, making an almost invisible dent on it while the inperceptible shockwaves running inside the wall weaken it nevertheless! Do our karma really have a proportionate effect or do they defy the established law of nature; that to every action, there is an equal and opposite reaction! In my realm of thought, I questioned myself, 'Was pain of remorse not a bigger punishment than confinement! Can mere confinement absolve one's crimes or purify souls? Can true remorse bring the criminal out and make it confront the corrupted souls? I could see that Sunder had served a life term in prison in last three days, rolling in pain and penitence on the dusty floors of his cell. I found no answers to any of my questions. I tried to catch sleep but my struggle to untangle the web of paradoxes kept me awake that night. I pondered to find my answers, to pacify me and to understand and come to terms with complexity of life!

Next morning I woke up after a short feverish spell of sleep, the photograph of Sunder's family photograph still clinging to my fingers. Looking at their smiling faces, I made up my mind.

The station in charge of the police station which controlled the red light district was an old friend. I called him and arrived at his office an hour later.

'Are you crazy?' He looked at me with bewilderment, 'is she connected to a case?' And without a lead, it is next to impossible!

'Rathore, this is far more important than that. Please do not ask any questions, just do it,' I insisted.

'Well, it is like searching a needle in a haystack; you know how cleverly they hide their prey and if they have already sold the woman, there are chances that she might be in another city by now. In that case, it would be even more difficult to trace her,' he was noncommittal.

'Do whatever it takes to dig her out, but you must rescue this woman, for my sake, please.' I pushed the photograph of Sunder's family in his palms and left; ignoring his protests!

In coming days I grew restless. There was no word from Rathore. I tried hard to forget Sunder's quandary and desperation, but those innocent faces kept haunting me. After almost two weeks, just a day before Sunder's next remand, Rathore called me. 'You are damn lucky, we have found the woman and also arrested a few men. If you want to meet her, come over before we move her to a safe house,' he sounded triumphant. Before he could hang the phone, I jumped from my chair and rushed to my car.

She was huddled in a corner in Rathore's cabin, flanked by two women from some NGO which would be sheltering her before being sent back to her home. I introduced myself meekly to the terrified woman. She looked devastated, ravaged by the events which had shaken her to the core. She raised her head, keeping her gaze low and asked in a feeble voice, laced with despair, 'Is he alright?'

'Yes; I will get you to meet him tomorrow, at the court,' I tried to assure her. I got no answer but a blank stare from a pair of moist and helpless eyes.

Next day, before Sunder arrived at the court, I was there, waiting for him. As soon as he stepped out from the van, he looked for me and found me standing near the entrance to the corridor of the building. He had shrunk even more than when I saw him last and his eyes were hollowed. I could see that those desperate eyes were asking me the same question a million times in a millionth of a second! I smiled at him and pointed to the bench in the corridor where Aditi sat, flanked by the volunteers. At first he could not see anything in the dimly lit patio, his eyes blinded by the glare of the sun. Then he saw her and ran almost dragging the constable with him. Kneeling at the bench where she sat, he cupped her face in his palms and cried. They wept over each other's shoulder for several minutes, occasionally looking at me with gratitude as if I was their saviour and not persecutor who had wrecked their lives.

I turned my eyes away; I had no courage to face their indebted stare.

Aditi left for Nepal a few days later after meeting Sunder in Jail. Sunder had pleaded with me to help her wife reach her home safely. I did see that she had a safe passage and even sent one of my trusted men to accompany her to the borders.

The verdict was pronounced a couple of months later. Sunder was sentenced to five years in prison. He had chosen not to appeal against the sentence which was strange as most would, but it was just two of us who knew the reason. Sunder had chosen to settle his score with his karma. By accepting the punishment, he wanted to reconcile with fate, to reap what he had sowed. His acceptance of the sentence was a tribute to his belief in fate and certitude of his destiny which he had chosen not to fight with!

That was the last day I saw Sunder. After pronouncement of the sentence, he came to me and stood before me for a moment, without uttering a single word and left in the jail van.

After about four years, I received a letter from him which was redirected several times before reaching me saying that he was released early for his good conduct in jail. He also wrote that before going back to his home, he had gone to my office to see me and requested an officer to convey his regards to me as I had relocated to Delhi.

Sunder sends me those greeting cards at every newyear eve with a new photograph of his family. I have never replied to or acknowledged them but this was one case which changed my view of life, crime and karma and the intricate mesh in which they are entwined in the matrix of actions and their repercussions.

I carefully slid the card and the photograph in the envelope and put it gently in my drawer.

* *

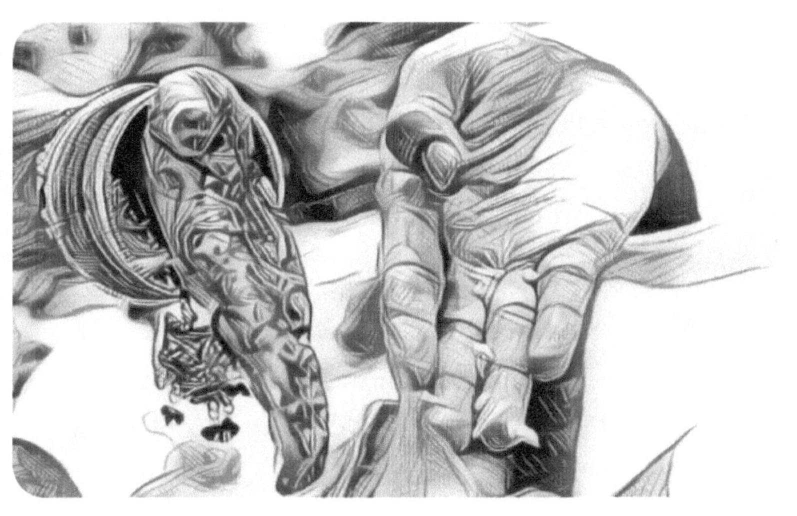

JHUMRU BHAIYA KI SHAADI

Weddings are made in heavens but at times, have to pass through the hell to reach the happy ending.

I put my foot down. 'No Dad, I am not going to that God forsaken village for wedding or whatsoever.' Dad raised his eyebrows, waiting for my first salvo of excuses.

'Did you forget that we have organized the seminar on 'gender inequality in rural India' in the collage and Danny's kitten's birthday bash is planned in cats' café next week! I can't miss all that fun!' I whined.

'Well, we have little choice; I will have to go and I am not leaving you alone here' Dad snapped. 'And Jhumru did come to attend your sister's wedding with his parents, didn't they? It will be very un courteous on our part if we do not attend his wedding.'

'But Dad, Didi's wedding was a destination wedding in Goa, and you sent their flight tickets too! And did you forget the ruckus they created there!' I tried to reason out.

It had happened that an awestruck Jhumru bhaiya, clad in a safari suit; was roaming on the Candolim beach when he approached a 'foreigner' bikini clad girl taking sun bath on the beach and insisted on a selfie with her. To his misfortune, her muscular companion lying next to her did not like his defiance when he ignored her refusal and insisted to pose with her! The furious guy got up and beat him black and blue; knocking him out. When Jhumru bhaiya, with a swollen eye and bruised lips; returned to the resort where the wedding was organized, his aghast father demanded a 'Tit for tat' revenge on the goon who had tormented his dear and 'innocent' son. It took quite an effort to pacify the agitated father who was ready to wage a war on the beach!

'And Dad, three days without wi fi! You know how bad the connectivity in remote areas is!' I tried my last weapon.

'What connectivity! Don't you think that connecting to your relatives is more important than your absurd social media!' He retorted with this favourite winning expression, 'After all I am your Dad.'

I surrendered.

We flew to Patna three days later from where we boarded a snail train to Motihari, a small town in Bihar where Jhumru bhaiya had arranged to pick us up; to be 'ferried' to his home in the village, a few miles away. After a six hours ride in an antique coach, sharing space with milk canisters, bicycles, a few sacks of dried cow dung cakes, even a couple of bleating goats and curious onlookers who kept on ogling at my pair of ripped jeans and 'extra' long hair; the train arrived at our destination. Although the halt was for a minute only, a grinning Jhumru bhaiya jumped inside the coach with a dozen of his friends who had come to welcome the '*Chote chacha*' from Mumbai.

He greeted Dad while I smiled and shouted 'Hi', much to dad's chagrin!

'Take your time, the train would not leave until you say so, we have removed the hose pipe.' He boasted; trying to flatter us; while I tried to make out what was a 'hose pipe'.

'Those chains are of no use,' he pointed to the emergency stop handles painted in red on the compartment wall in scorn. 'We break the hose pipes between the wagons, so that it takes minimum ten minutes to fix that before the train can move,' he boasted with triumph.

I acknowledged his valour with a nod and picked up my suitcase.

"No you don't have to,' he shouted at his accomplices who hurriedly snatched the luggage from us and escorted us out of the coach; on the cold gravelled platform. By this time, the hapless guard and the motorman had arrived near the wagon and were trying to reconnect the vacuum hose; looking at us with helpless scorn. Jhumru bhaiya smiled at them and gestured to one of his cronies to give them the missing nut of the vacuum pipe they had opened. Then he led our little convoy out of the station where our 'transport' was waiting.

'Do not worry *babu*; this is the only thing which can travel to our village; we do not have good roads like in Delhi and Mumbai', he laughed at my bewildered face and threw our suitcases onto the trailer of a tractor!

I was aghast! I looked at Dad for support but he was too excited with the prospect of travelling onto a tractor; gleefully caressing the rickety vehicle which must have been salvaged from the scrap yard!

'Eicher, 1964 model, all German, full metal body and single carburettor! Who can believe that they still run! These machines were used by even our military in the Indo China war! Amazing!' He was mesmerized; marvelling at the piece of junk! He was an automobile engineer and had a weak spot in his heart for such medieval pieces retrieved from their graveyards!

Miles away from his fascination, I pondered over my option of travelling six kilometres in freezing cold on that war relic!

'You two would be sitting here, Jhumru bhaiya showed us our seats besides him while he jumped on to the driver's saddle. Rest of the boys jumped on to the trailer. After many attempts and curses, the cold and sluggish engine began chugging; spewing black fumes from almost everywhere; exhaust pipe included. He grinned in triumph and drove.

After going for a little over a mile, every bone in my body was rattling! The narrow tar road which had perhaps not seen repairs for ages was pockmarked with potholes; some as big and deep as an aquarium! Later I tweeted to my friends,' Guys, forget that dharna before the BMC office we planned against the bad roads; first come and see these; we have potholes in Mumbai and these roads have craters!'

'The roads are still better here; just wait for the last mile, there is no road! That was washed away in last year's rains; Jhumru bhaiya said.

'But before the next election, all these roads would be smooth and shine like Hema Malini's cheeks!' He mimicked the infamous remarks of an ex Chief Minister of Bihar about the roads he had built in Patna before he was jailed in a scam!

After almost an hour of horrendous drive, we reached the sleepy village amidst nowhere; a ghetto of some hundred odd houses of different shapes and sizes; a few made of bricks. Alerted by the sound of the tractor, a stray buffalo stopped in her tracks and bellowed loudly; announcing our arrival. The streets were barren; except a few men wrapped in blankets and carrying water panes lazily strolling to the open lands to relieve themselves. Most of the villagers were cocooned inside in the warmth of their homes; they would come out when the sun shines and go to the farms to work or gather in the village square to discuss crops and politics over the fumes of *hookah* and *bidis.* Navigating our way through the narrow spiral streets; full of muck and dazed goats and buffaloes, we arrived at Jhumru bhaiya's home.

Vishnu uncle; Dad's elder cousin, came out and stood in the patio. I could not make much out of him as he was covered from head to toe in a blanket; exposing only his nostrils and eyes. Behind the half open door to the interiors, I could see a few curious feminine faces who had scrambled to see the '*shahari babus'* from Mumbai.

'Welcome to *Chatarpur*! He gave a loud shout in English which I suspected was well practised for this moment. I got down from the tractor; nursing my sore backside! Dad coaxed me to touch his feet before I could utter 'Hi'. Vishnu uncle stretched his arms covered in blanket; looking like a giant bat, ready to fly with it's open wings and embraced Dad while I pretended to touch his knees and stood at a safe distance. Then he turned to me; looking at the tears of my ragged jeans and said with a genuine concern, 'Did you fall somewhere?'

I ignored his remarks and went to the boys who were unloading our stuff from the trailer while dad explained the latest trend of ragged jeans to him; popular among youths in cities. Vishnu uncle nodded pensively and blabbered how the values of youth in cities had deteriorated while the villages still preserved the Indian culture.

'You can feel the difference in air here when you breath.' He boasted, standing near a huge methane emitting mound of cow dung.

'Here everything is fresh, pure and organic,' He claimed and led us to our room which was dark and smelt of mould. There was no power.

'Lights would come back by evening; in any case it is not necessary in the day time,' He said casually while I frantically jostled with my cell phone, searching for network. There was none.

This was the first of the three days of the wedding ceremony which began with '*Tilak*'. At the breakfast table Dad explained the ritual, 'This evening, the guys from the bride side would come with the dowry and present to the groom, and there will be puja and the feast.'

'The youth of today hardly know about our 'grand' traditions; wait for the next generation and see,' Vishnu uncle lamented; looking at my long curls with a contemptuous glance.

Once back in our room which had a window as small as those in prison cells, I confronted dad, 'Dowry! Why dowry? We did not give anything as such on didi's wedding, did we?'

'That was different,' He meant to say it was a love marriage, so no dowry.

'Well, here if you are looking for a groom, you must arrange a dowry first; jewellery, a car or two wheeler, household goods and cash to secure a groom. The quantum would depend on the job and antecedents of the groom and family assets etc.' He explained!

'What does Jhumru bhaiya do? A good job?'I doubted he was well educated!

Dad laughed and said, 'No, he is jobless; failed in his higher secondary examinations. Your uncle supports him; but he is lucky to get this girl as wife. She is a post graduate!' Her father could not afford a groom with good job as the dowry would be too high, so they settled for Jhumru.' Dad clarified.

'So what dowry Jhumru bhaiya is getting?' I was curious.

'No idea, we can see that in the evening itself when their people come with the presents. ' Dad assured me.

After a while we freshened up and had our 'organic' meal. On the dining table, Vishnu uncle explained what a 'swindler' the bride's father was who had been haggling over 'small' things in dowry like the scooter which was promised but 'fraudulently' replaced with a cheap moped and had also reduced the amount of cash initially agreed upon. On top of that, he had also gone back on his promise of serving mutton and fish for the wedding party! He rued.

'What a miser! If they could not afford, he could have looked for another groom, no?' He looked at my father for affirmation.

'You wait and see what they bring today! Jhumru is also very upset about the scooter which I had promised him!' He was worried about his dear son!

A band began blaring at the door well before the sunset where the invitees had been gathering. They sat in small groups; men and women separately, under a large multicolour marquee. While the elders blew out acrid smoke from their *hookahs*, children ran around in excitement around the table where soft drinks were being served. Women in their colourful *sarees* and glittering jewellery sat in groups and gossiped in hushed tone about Jhumru's bride and his dowry while Vishnu uncle went around the crowd; greeting people and explaining the 'deceit' of the bride's family.

The entourage from the bride's side arrived in a white suv which was immediately surrounded by the curious children. The bride's father and a few male relatives got down from the vehicle, carrying boxes, bags, cartons and brand new suitcases. Soon after, a small truck followed on which a two wheeler was loaded, covered in tarpaulin. The excited bunch of Jhumru bhaiya's friends unloaded the two wheeler and removed the tarpaulin. It was a brand new *Bajaj* scooter. Jhumru bhaiya gasped with disbelief at the sight of the scooter!

'How can we displease our son in law!' The bride's father, an old and haggard man in his seventies beamed with pride and wrapped his hand around Jhumru bhaiya's shoulder who was flabbergasted by seeing the scooter! 'But *damadji*, believe me, I had to mortgage my last piece of land for this,' He pointed out to the gleaming blue scooter, wrapped in cellophane. Jhumru bhaiya looked at his would be father in law with gratitude and whispered, 'Papa was telling me that you have halved the cash we had agreed upon!'

The old man hung his head in shame and pleaded, 'son, this is the best I could do; I am almost broke, all for the sake of my daughter.'

The ceremony began; led by a *pundit* who kept each item of the dowry; the keys of the scooter included, one by one on the palms of Jhumru bhaiya who sat on the ground, clad in traditional attire; seeking divine approval to the extortion. A relative of the bride gave a brief commentary explaining each item of dowry and cash including the scooter's brand and price to the audience. After that, the *pundit* chanted mantras and invited the men from the bride side to put sandal paste on Jhumru bhaiya's forehead, thus sealing the alliance. Once this was over, the dinner followed where Vishnu uncle had arranged to serve fish and mutton.

'We will show them that we are not beggars like them,' He said to my father. 'They have no class, you see,' He boasted, pointing to the cauldron of mutton curry.

The ceremony had ended and the guests had departed. The lights had gone out again, leaving the entire village in dark. Tired and frustrated by the bone breaking tractor ride and the erratic mobile network, I pulled my blanket over my head and fell asleep almost immediately. Dad who was invited to the 'exclusive' group of elders which had sat in an ante room; drinking 'English wine' before the dinner, snored loudly besides me.

We woke up in the morning by the sounds of the wailing of Jhumru bhaiya's mother and frantic shouts of Vishnu uncle. Still dazed, I shook dad who was happily snoring, unaware of the storm in the house. When he woke up, we ran out to the courtyard where the aunt was beating her chest while Jhumru bhaiya and Vishnu uncle sat on the floor; heads hung on their chests.

'What happened?' My father shouted.

Without raising his head, Jhumru bhaiya pointed to a room along the courtyard, with doors ajar.

Fearing the worst, we ran inside the windowless room and saw a big gaping hole in the wall which opened onto the backyard, filling the room with sunshine. Puzzled, we came back to Jhumru bhaiya.

'There is nothing but a big hole,' I was confused.

'Everything is gone, even the scooter, and the cash and jewellery too, Vishnu uncle lamented; stroking his forehead. Apparently, the thieves had burgled in; removing the bricks in the aged wall and fled with the booty which was widely publicised last evening in the '*tilak*' ceremony. Suddenly, the entire house had plunged into gloom. The women beat their chests and the groom's blissful life plunged into darkness, just before it was to begin. The family mourned the loss of assets which it had never earned!

Somewhere deep in my heart, I was greatly relieved while dad went into a brain storming session with Jhumru bhaiya and Vishnu uncle over the next course of action. In the afternoon, Vishnu uncle took a resolution.

"We would cancel the wedding unless we get the dowry back; either from the thieves or from them.' He meant the bride's family. The *pundit* who had doubled up as the matrimonial agent was summoned and given the verdict; to convey to the bride's father.

He returned in the evening with the 'bad' news that the bride's father had conveyed his sympathies but refused to replenish a single rupee.

This brought more heartache for the family; Jhumru bhaiya in particular, who had been dreaming of romantic rides on the scooter with his new bride, her arms wrapped around his waist, taking her to the city to see movies and shop with the booty from the dowry.

That day the house remained abuzz with police men and sympathetic villagers who speculated about the theft and the lawlessness in the area while the family elders brooded over the prospects of wedding. Somehow my father and other elders convinced Vishnu uncle to go ahead with the wedding as cancellation would bring 'bad' name to the family.

'The matter of dowry can be sorted later; after all their girl will have to live in this house.' The village *sarpanch* asserted with a menacing threat directed at the bride!

So next day in the evening, the wedding procession started. Vishnu uncle had cancelled the lights and the band since the money to be paid to them was gone. Dad had forced me to replace my favourite ragged jeans and hoody with traditional ensemble which I hated. Obviously it was Vishnu uncle who had objected at my 'torn' clothes which could tarnish his reputation!

The procession of a hundred odd men and boys travelled in a convoy of tractors and a lone suv wherein the groom and select family members travelled with us; literally jumping our way to the bride's place, some ten miles away on non existent roads. Everyone remained silent; drowned in melancholy. After almost an hour of negotiating the terrain, we arrived at a decrepit building of the middle school; our 'guest house' in the village which was arranged by the bride's father. With horror, I refused to believe that this was the place where we would spend the night. The building could crash any moment; window panes were missing and there were gaping holes in the tiled roof. The place stunk of cow dung and moist hey which was strewn everywhere; in fact our beds were made of the mattresses of hey and foul smelling blankets. Apparently the bitter remarks flying from the war of the words had permeated to the bride's family; or the broke father could not afford any place better. I could see the bitterness and animosity on the faces of '*baratis*' who were aghast at the show of such poor hospitality by the bride's side. Vishnu uncle and Jhumru bhaiya were almost at the breaking point; burning with anger and frustration!

After an hour or so while everyone freshened up and got ready for the wedding ritual at the bride's house which was nearby, I enthusiastically tweeted about the situation and posted photographs of our 'accommodation'. Unlike others, I was happy and liked this village; at least the mobile data network here was excellent!

We walked to the house, led by a band arranged by the bride's father which played out of tune Hindi film songs. The house was decked up for the occasion with lights and colourful flags. A large marquee stood in the front where a loudspeaker blared the song, '*Bambai se aaya mera dost....*' as our procession arrived at the house. Ladies in bright attires came forward to the car and performed *aarti* of Jhumru bhaiya who remained morose and kept his head hung. Thereafter the buoyant women escorted him to the wedding altar; singing folk songs while we sat on plastic chairs under the marquee, braving the chilling wind and mosquitoes. After a while, the bride arrived; escorted by her giggling friends and sat beside the groom but Jhumru bhaiya did not look at her; maintaining his pensive mood. The priest began the rituals and after an hour of chanting mantras, he announced the beginning of the '*pheras*. But just before it was to begin, Vishnu uncle approached the jubilant father of the bride and told him that the *pheras* would start only after he promises to replenish the dowry.

As his words spread, a pin drop silence swept over the place followed by hushed up murmurs and then to shouts and angry words from both the sides; reaching a crescendo! I hurriedly hid behind dad who remained neutral; probably in a dilemma of which side he should take! The situation was palpitating as the war of words escalated. The hapless mother of the bride began crying; embracing her daughter who had gotten up at the altar. Then suddenly everyone froze with the sound of a gunshot which was probably fired in air, outside the marquee. A moment later, a burly man who looked ferocious, entered the marquee with a double barrel gun, it's muzzle still oozing smoke. He was bride's maternal uncle, the *Mamaji* whom I recognised as he was the part of the entourage for the '*Tilak*' ceremony. He walked to the altar with the gun and stood near the terror stricken Jhumru bhaiya who had also got up. He put his massive hand on his shoulder, gesturing him with his menacing eyes to sit down and begin the *pheras*. Jhumru bhaiya promptly obeyed his command without bothering to seek his father's approval and took *pheras* with the shaken bride around the sacred fire. After that, the *pundit* prompted Jhumru bhaiya to put vermilion on the bride's head who was now his legal wife; which he obeyed with a forced smile on his face. The emboldened women immediately began singing wedding songs with renewed gusto while all of us including Vishnu uncle stood frozen inhaling the insult and smoke from the fire in the altar.

While all this was happening, Vishnu uncle crawled to Dad and whispered, 'Enough is enough! This is *goondagardi!* We are not taking this insult lying down, are we?'

Dad looked at him with uncertainty. It was not the time to show bravery, that too in face of a gun and hundreds of hostile villagers!

"Boycott their food, we would not touch even a single drop of their water!' He had found the solution in Gandhiji's 'satyagrah.'

I hurriedly hid my coke behind my back while Vishnu uncle went around and whispered his verdict to the hungry folks on our side; waiting for the fill, to their dismay. Then he tottered to the bride's father and conveyed his decision who immediately passed it onto his brother in law with the gun who was apparently calling the shots now.

The dictate of Vishnu uncle further enraged *Mamaji*. He cocked his gun and fired again in the air, making a hole in the roof of the marquee while we scrambled to take cover.

'So you want to insult by refusing to eat?' He roared. 'And what would happen to the food which is prepared for you; throw them down the drain?' He threatened Vishnu uncle; tapping his gun!

The verdict was clear. The *baratis*, who were more worried for their hungry bellies than their self esteem, welcomed the happy ending and rushed to the tables where a cold dinner waited for them. Gulping the chilled dal, I tweeted, 'Folks; this is unreal! You have heard food being snatched on gunpoint but ever seen forced to eat with a gun on your head!' Undeterred, Vishnu uncle had refused to eat; citing his fasting for this 'pious' occasion. Meanwhile, the buoyant friends of the bride had stolen Jhumru bhaiya's shoes and refused to return unless he gave them five thousand rupees. Once the deal was settled at one thousand rupees, they filled his mouth with puries and sweets before returning the shoes.

Humiliated and defeated, we prepared to leave the venue and reached our 'guesthouse' which was dark and cold. It was well past midnight. I tried to sleep but mosquitoes and frantic conversation of the elders kept me awake.

Early morning we went to the bride's home to take the bride and Jhumru bhaiya who was almost a dignified hostage. The burly *Mamaji*, sans his gun; and much sombre by now, welcomed us and offered us tea and snacks which pacified Vishnu uncle to some extent who was piqued by his insolent behaviour last night. *Mamaji* came forward with a wide grin and held Vishnu uncle in a rib breaking embrace and whispered in a voice which sounded as a request and threat at the same time. 'Priya is our dearest girl, so please take good care of her.' Vishnu uncle nodded and forced an awkward smile on his face.

The bride and an upbeat Jhumru bhaiya appeared from the door; followed by the women who cried with the pain of parting away from their girl. The band waiting outside began howling the tune of '*Babul ki duayen leti jaa, ja tujhko sukhi sasnsar mile.......*' while we along with the newlywed couple got inside the vehicle and drove to the school where others were waiting to follow us back to our village. The wedding had ended.

We took the afternoon train to the city and subsequently our flight to Mumbai where I nursed the mosquito bites for days while savouring the hilarious experience of the wedding.

It was not before a couple of years while we braved the pandemic; dad told me that Vishnu uncle was gravely sick and was being flown to Mumbai for treatment.

Next day, we went to the airport to pick them up from where Vishnu uncle was taken to the hospital and admitted. Jhumru bhaiya and his wife; *Priya bhabhi* had accompanied him. After Vishnu uncle was taken to the ICU, we waited in the hospital corridor and chatted.

I was dying to know what might have happened to *Priya bhabhi* in Jhumru bhaiya's home after the showdown. 'Was she tortured, maltreated for dowry?'

So I decided to talk to Jhumru bhaiya in private about the last two years of their lives.

'Initially Papa and Mummy both were hostile to her but as time went by, I found no fault of hers in the episode that happened at the wedding. We never got back the stuff which was stolen but just six months after the wedding, she gave me money to buy the scooter! At first I suspected that her father had sent the money but I was wrong! And she was the one who coaxed me to work with Papa at the court so that I could learn work and stand on my own feet! After finishing the house chores, she would sit in front of the computer while I went for work. Ma had been furious for Priya would stick to the computer for hours but despite that she never misbehaved with any of us! We all realized her true worth last month when Papa became ill and we needed money for the treatment. When we had lost all hopes, she came to me and gave me two lakhs rupees which she had been saving from some on line teaching job.' Jhumru bhaiya narrated; stealing fondly glances at her wife.

Do you know what she said? 'I only wanted my father's head high and not hung in shame, so I was saving this money to repay his debt ; but right now my father in law's life is the top priority!' If papa lives, the credit would go to her,' He asserted fondly; in a voice choking with emotions and love for his wife.

A week later, Vishnu uncle was discharged and came to our home where he recuperated for a few more days while Priya bhabhi tirelessly attended to his needs, spoon feeding him and giving his medicines, even washing his soiled clothes!

In another week, he was back on his feet; ready to go home. Before leaving, he called everyone in the living room where we all sat; while Priya bhabhi served us tea and snacks.

'Priya, come here,' the old man called her and patted her head affectionately.

"I am indebted to you with my life my child, and now, in front of everyone, I beg forgiveness for how we treated you and your father! From today onwards, you are my daughter and not daughter in law,' Vishnu uncle uttered lovingly as tears rolled down his eyes.

* *

ELIXIR OF LIFE

Friendship in it's purest form is beyond all virtues and above all the lures.

At the far side of the great ridge beyond the mountains in west where the sun embraced earth at dusk; stood a humble chalet. Its wooden walls had withered with age and the roof made of dried hay had holes made by hailstorms. A few smaller dwellings made of mud and grass roof dotted around it; like ducklings in attention to their mother. The fearless habitants of the settlement had not cared to fence the compound; for even the beasts from the forest respected them and the sanctity of the place. It was a *gurukul,* the quintessence of wisdom and spiritual attainment, a monastery where streams of knowledge and faith flew in abundance like water in the river which drifted from the hills in its backyard.

Untying the bundle of firewood, Shivank called for his friend, Daksh, another disciple in the *gurukul* who was cleaning the ground for setting up the hearth where supper would be cooked for the *Guru* and other inmates.

'We have little grains in the store today but I think, we can manage with whatever is left, can't we Daksh?' Shivank sounded worried.

'Yes Shivank, we can. Did not we learn from *Guruji* today that *Ajivikas* followers abhorred hoarding of any kind and consumed minimum and though they defied Vedas, they enlightened us on how to seek happiness in frugality,' Daksh laughed and ignited the hearth.

Shivank and Daksh were friends and soul mates, like one life in two physical bodies. They had come to this convent together from the same village and were adored by their *Guru* and revered by all the other disciples in the *gurukul*. The monastery nurtured their bonding and truthfulness to each other in its purest form, an embodiment of a truth embracing another, satiated and inseparable.

Their days passed in that temple of wisdom, learning and preparing for the next stage of their lives with other pupils before the day came when their revered *Guru* was to give them '*Diksha*', the consecration to prepare them for their ascetic life and become apostles of consciousness and wisdom. On that auspicious day, after the morning prayers; he summoned all the pupils dressed in white loin clothes who sat around the holy fire. Thereafter *Guruji* consecrated them one after another by chanting mantras in front of the sacred fire while the other disciples sang Vedic hymns amidst the gentle sound of the river and fragrant fumes of incense sticks.

After all the pupils took *Diksha* except Shivank and Daksh, the *Guru* called Shivank and purified him by sprinkling water from the holy rivers and placing his sandal smeared palm on his crown, chanting mantras. Then he took out a small copper vessel from the altar which was sealed and placed it in his folded palms.

'This is only for the purest and highest of the souls; *Amrit*, the elixir of life.' He said amidst gasps and murmur of disbelief and applause from the disciples.

'You are my most valued disciple. Upon drinking this potion, Gods will bestow on you divine health and vigour, and a life to last forever. I wish you serve the human kind with the power; for Gods have chosen you to spread light and the eternal truth.' He continued, 'Remember, this potion is not to be shared, otherwise it will no longer remain *amrit* but turn into ordinary water.'

Then turning to Daksh he said,' My child, your learning is not yet over, therefore you are serving this ashram for some more time.'

The ceremony had ended, leaving everyone puzzled as Daksh was the only one who was not consecrated.

All the disciples dispersed, rejoicing at the thought of joining their families but Shivank and Daksh sat through the day huddled together and spell bound. The agony of separation had snatched their words. In last few years of togetherness, they had not imagined a world devoid of each other.

The next morning, the jubilant pupils left home after paying their respect to the *Guruji* and so did Shivank, albeit with a heart laden with sorrow and remorse.

He held Daksh in his embrace and whispered in his ears with tear laden eyes, 'I shall be waiting for you.' Then he left, dragging himself away.

But Shivank had no plans to go back to his home. Not very far away from the *gurukul,* on the other side of the ridge, he made a small hut of twigs and dried leaves and waited for his companion. Months passed and finally the day came when Daksh was called by *Guruji* and purified with holy verses. The *Guru* blessed and consecrated him.

Daksh paid his homage and *gurudakshina* to his Master and left the monastery. He knew that his friend, whom he had not seen since he left, would be waiting for him somewhere close. In a while, he found him in his makeshift hut with a small Banyan tree in its courtyard. Shivank had turned pale and feeble, his eyes were hollow in their sockets and his fragile body looked ravaged by hunger and the wait. They embraced and cried silently, rejoicing and savouring the re union.

'How you have become so weak, my friend. Was not the potion meant to give you good health and vigour and keep you robust?' Daksh asked him with concern and fear for his friend who looked devastated.

Shivank, who was overwhelmed on seeing his second self, smiled and said, 'How can I be selfish my brother! We all know that you deserved that potion more than me, or anyone in the ashram! I have kept it safe, waiting for you to claim! He picked up the cauldron of *amrit* and offered to Daksh.

Daksh was spell bound.

'No my brother, you are the chosen one and it is you who truly deserves this elixir and who would be happier than me if you become immortal!' Daksh refused.

Shivank smiled and looked at Daksh, 'My dear friend, had not we pledged to live a life together; like brothers from the same womb and vowed to remain one! Are not we bound by our oath of sharing happiness and misery equally and face life and death with the same breath of ours! If this elixir of life is meant for only one of us, I would prefer death to immortality or any other virtue of this universe.

They came out with the copper pot to the Holy *Banyan* tree Shivank had grown in front of the hut.

'I had sown this sapling the day I came here, to mark our togetherness and sacred friendship. Let it grow and live forever, for it would be the denotation for our friendship and apostle of peace and harmony.' Shivank smiled. Daksh nodded and they held the cauldron of eternal life together and poured the '*Amrit*' in the roots of the Banyan tree.

* *

BLESSINGS

A beggar came to me and gave his blessings; asking for alms and I refused. Am I not indebted to him?

On a hot summer day, a group of beggars waited on the sidewalk near a busy intersection for the vehicles to stop. As the signal lights turned red, they would get up and rush to the waiting cars, tapping window panes for alms and come back to their place.

Among those beggars sat a battered old woman with a pair of crutches by her sides. Although wrecked by miseries and a bent back, she had a tranquil composure and looked satiated. Unlike other beggars, she would get up only once in a while painstakingly, to beg and return without grimace even if she got nothing or very little.

After a while, when the lights turned red, the old woman gathered her crutches and limped to a big shiny car and tapped the window pane. The man at the wheel who looked opulent in his expensive suite, was visibly irritated by the distraction and avoided looking at her through the glass. The old woman repeated the tap which she normally won't do.

The man, apparently irked, rolled down the window pane and stared angrily at the woman. The beggar smiled and said 'God bless you my son.'

He shouted angry words at her and drove away.

A few days later, the same car stopped at that crossroad. The old lady again tottered to the car on her crutches and tapped the window.

'God have mercy on you, may all the happiness be yours', she said. It was the same man in his fancy suite, laden with worries of life and its intricacies. He looked at the woman with scorn and shouted 'Stop nagging, I am not giving anything to you' and drove away.

The beggar returned to her place and sat down on the sidewalk with a calm and complacent composure. Another beggar, sitting by her side who had been watching her, asked, 'That haggard is useless, he won't give anything. Why don't you try someone else instead?'

The old woman smiled and said 'Well, did you look at him! Don't you think that he needs my blessings more than I need his coins?'

* *

A GUEST IN WILDERNESS

Generosity is not the virtue of rich alone; it is embedded in poverty, like a pearl inside an oyster and thus, closer to Godliness.

In remote hinterlands amidst deep forests, lived a poor farmer with his family. The surrounding mountains had scant population and his means were very limited. One evening, when he and his family sat for supper after a hard day's work, someone knocked the door of their humble abode. The farmer got up and opened the door to find a ravaged man, sick and hungry. His unkempt hair hung on his sunken shoulders and his lips were white and cracked with thirst. Barely able to stand, the famished man with trembling breath leaned at the door frame with much effort and looked at the farmer with feverish eyes. He whispered some words which were barely audible.

'Please come inside and settle down, you are too weak,' the farmer held his fragile hands and escorted him to their board where the family was about to begin their supper. There was not much on the table as the harvesting had not yet begun and their granary was almost empty. The man sat and hurriedly began eating while the farmer's wife and children stood behind him, serving water and whatever food was left.

'I came from beyond those mountains, searching for game but was attacked by wild animals and lost my food and weapons,' he pointed his finger in direction of the closed window.

After finishing the last grain on the table, the man raised his head and looked at the children in attendance.

'Oh, how cruel I am! Forgive me for I ate all the food you had. Gods will punish me for your family would sleep hungry tonight,' the ashamed man lamented with extreme self- mortification.

The poor farmer smiled at him and said, 'Gods have rewarded you with your life so how could They punish you! And the same Gods who showed you the way to my home, would take care of my family too. But had I not brought you in, whom could you go to in this wilderness!'

Then the farmer offered him his blanket and a warm bed.

* *

147

In loving memories of my mother.

www.ingramcontent.com/pod-product-compliance
Lightning Source LLC
Chambersburg PA
CBHW031143130726
47988CB00006B/2504